Protecting Her

By Carmen Lace

WARNING: This book contains sexually explicit scenes and adult language. It may be considered offensive to some readers. This book is intended for adults 18+ ONLY. Please ensure this book is stored somewhere that cannot be accessed by underage readers.

Message from the Author:

Thank you so much for downloading my book! I hope you will enjoy it as much as I did writing it. After reading, please give the book your honest feedback by submitting an Amazon review. It would take just a few moments and will mean the world to me to hear my reader's feedback. I hope to deliver many more books and truly thankful I'm able to write for my audience. Please visit my website and subscribe to my newsletter where I announce new books coming out and give out free promotions/books (I do not spam and have total respect to my subscribers). Read more about me at the end of the book.

Download one of my other books for FREE:
http://carmenlace.com/giveaway

Contents

Introduction

Fresh out of the Police Academy in Hartford, Connecticut, Serena Blake is an idyllic 21-year-old following in her deceased brother's footsteps. As a rookie, she's assigned to patrol with a veteran of her division until she learns the ropes.

Her partner is Darcy Fairweather, a no-nonsense and moody lesbian who's hard to impress. Luckily, Serena is a very impressive rookie. The two find themselves becoming fast friends and more.

Before too long, Serena is allowed to patrol on her own. While answering an emergency call, she takes exactly all the right actions to make herself a hero. However, something goes wrong and she finds herself incriminated instead. It's up to Darcy to find out how to put everything right and clear Serena's name. There's a mystery to solve, and a lot of questions that need answering. Most importantly, what will they become to each other?

Chapter One

818 hours. That was the amount required in order to be able to take the final Academy assessment. That was 8 hours a day, 7 days a week, for a grand total of 14 weeks. Never in her entire life did Serena ever work at something as hard as she had while in the Academy. That was probably because she'd never been very passionate about anything else.

She'd never taken a single sport or been part of a single extracurricular activity in her entire life, and she sure as heck hadn't cared about her schooling like that. She had gone into this a completely blank slate and come out with flying colors. At least that was what the instructors all said at the very end, after admitting that they thought at the end of each day that they'd never see her again.

Serena was pretty sure she'd been right there along with them, dragging her sore and sorry ass home each night with the thought in her mind that none of this was going to ever be worth it. Living, breathing, eating, studying cop life just wasn't all it was cracked up to me.

But the thing was, she hadn't expected it to be.

A tentative little smile played around the corners of her mouth as she headed out of her apartment and strode rapidly down the few flights of stairs to reach the ground floor. Practically flinging herself out the door, she hurried over to her beat up old truck where it was parked on the grass. A ferociously cold wind blew, knifing through the trees to stab her anywhere her skin was exposed. Shivering, Serena tugged her scarf a little higher and then jumped into the truck. The locks on the doors didn't work, which wasn't exactly an ideal thing when Hartford was overrun with crime lately and her apartment was in a backwoodsy corner on the outskirts of the city, but she had been lucky so far.

She had always been lucky, even when she wasn't. She was just one of those kinds of people.

Smiling broader now, she started up the engine, let it warm up a bit and defrost the tiny bit of chill which had settled on the windshield in the night. Then, she headed out along the curvy little road. A few sharp turns later and suddenly she was veering sharply across a four-lane stretch of road in the city in the heart of Connecticut.

Well, not exactly the heart. Hartford wasn't the capital. But it was the most important in her heart, because she'd grown up here. Never lived anywhere else. The winding Connecticut River fueled her drifting dreams, and the parks fed her childhood imagination. Later on in life, both were great places to hang out and fuck in secrecy. There were museums here, art galleries abound, restaurants from all her favorite cultures – where could she ever want to go but here?

And now, just as Hartford sheltered her, she was going to shelter it.

A short ten minutes later, a commute which should have been half that if not for traffic, and she was pulling up in front of the Police Department. The building was nothing much to look at from the standpoint of a passerby –official buildings like this never were- but to her it was the greatest thing she'd ever seen. The little arch above the doorway, the only trace of grandeur in such an otherwise underwhelming place, seemed to her to be a grand portal to the rest of her life.

Heart swelling with pride, Serena parked her truck in one of the spaces designated for officers only, got out, and headed inside.

The interior was just as underwhelming as the outside. Immediately to the left there was a broad expanse of brown counter, while to the right there was a waiting area with an open floor and a few rows of uncomfortable plastic seats. Various doors and windows positioned elsewhere led deeper into the station, offering glimpses of officers passing by or the technical rooms beyond which she might someday soon get to enter.

A man stood behind the counter, fiddling idly with a pad of paper and a pen. His cheek rested on his hand, while his uniform hung limp around his body as though it was trying to leave him behind in disgust.

His eyes turned towards her while the rest of him stayed static. Only that and the rise and fall of his chest showed that he was anything more than a statue.

Good first impression, sir, Serena thought. No wonder his two-sizes-too-big uniform looked like it was running away from him.

“What can I help you with, ma’am?” the officer droned.

He wasn’t going to ruin her good mood, no way. Smiling at him, she said, “I just graduated from the Academy. Today is my very first day, and I was told to come here at 8 a.m.”

The officer straightened up a little to glance at the clock on the nearby wall. When he did that, the folds of his uniform straightened out a little to reveal his nametag. Chad, it said. Of course. He felt like a Chad to her, that was for sure.

"It's 7:50 a.m."

"Well...Yes. But I wanted to get here early!"

"One of those, are you?" Chad snorted, and then glanced at her up and down like it was the first time he was really seeing her.

Serena shook her head. "I'm not sure what you mean by that." The unspoken part was that she was pretty damn sure that she *did* know what he meant, and she didn't like it. Hopefully he would feel like an idiot if he had to explain. Not the best way to start out her day at a new job, at the only job she'd ever had, but she wasn't a pushover.

"Chad, I'm pretty sure I didn't put you behind the counter for you to harass anyone who comes in."

Both Serena and Chad turned in the direction of the new voice. A short, round black woman stood there, hanging halfway out of a doorway. Her head was close-shaven so all that remained was little more than a fuzz of black curls, and her posture was severe.

“Sorry, boss,” Chad said, in a tone of voice which sounded exactly like a shrug.

The uniformed woman sighed and stepped out fully into the open. “Actually, I’m starting to think that you can’t even survive behind the counter, but unless I put you on janitor duties you can’t get any lower on the ladder. Hell, you aren’t even bright enough to be a lamp.”

Chad put up his hands and laughed good-humoredly, though his eyes sparked with just a tiny bit of resentment. “You got me, boss. Okay.”

“Good.” The woman turned to face Serena now, the motion perfectly clear as a dismissal. Serena was taken in by the structure of her face, which was full and impressive without any hair to obscure a single part of it. Her cheeks were broad, her chin a little too defined, and her eyebrows could have used some of the trimming that she’d done on her hair, but the eyes beneath them were kind enough. “I take it you’re Serena Blake, then?”

Serena nodded, abruptly aware of her own long hair swishing around when she did. “Yes, ma’am.”

“It’s a pleasure to have you here,” the woman said, and smiled genuinely. “My name is Catherine Jacobs. I’m the Lieutenant in charge of your division.”

Serena reached out and shook her hand. “It’s an honor to meet you, Lieutenant,” she said. As she withdrew her hand, she felt something move against her palm and looked down to see what it could possibly be. It was a hair tie.

“I’m glad. Now, put up your hair. Bun, not a pony.”

A little mystified, Serena did exactly as asked. When she was done, the Lieutenant took off at a fierce pace that seemed to belie her short legs. “Tomorrow, you’ll have that done before you leave your house. You’re very pretty and I don’t care what anyone does with their appearance, but when you’re on the force, letting your hair stay like that is a huge risk to your safety."

"I understand." A little miffed at having already screwed up, Serena said, "It won't happen again," and she meant it. She was resolved to be the best. That meant learning from her mistakes.

"It better not," Lieutenant Jacobs said. They headed down one of the nearby halls and began a quick and yet exhaustive tour of the rooms. Interrogation, break room, bathrooms, offices, cubicle land and a small two-bunk area where any officers could stay if for some reason they needed to. Serena shivered a little with anticipation as they passed the holding cells. They were currently empty but it was only Tuesday. Part of her knew that by the end of the week, they'd be packed with drunk and rowdy jerks who got a little too in over their heads.

All through the tour, they constantly passed by other officers. Serena greeted each one in kind and shook their hands as firmly as she could. The men greatly outnumbered the women, but seemed a lot friendlier towards her.

Before too long, they ended up right back where they were before but just off that main room, in a dimly-lit corner near a storage closet.

"Well," the Lieutenant said, "that's about it for our lovely station. Not as grand as some others –ever been to NYC?- but it does what it has to do."

"I think it's perfect."

The Lieutenant snorted. "Heh. Somehow, I almost think you really mean that. Just wait, though. Once the newness of it wears off, you'll be wishing you went to law school or someplace that's actually interesting. Anyway, what size are you? Need to get you into a proper uniform."

Putting on that uniform was like a dream come true. Mentally, that was. Physically, the material didn't breathe very well and it was scratchy, and it practically squeaked whenever she moved because it was so new, but she loved it. This was a sign that she had really, truly made it. Everything paid off in that moment, when she finished buttoning the last button.

“Looks good on you,” the Lieutenant said. The corner of her mouth quirked a little as she said it, even though she was obviously trying to keep a straight face.

Serena laughed. “Somehow, I don’t think you’re telling the truth.”

“I don’t think it really flatters anyone. Now, your piece.”

The process of signing out and being issued a standard pistol took a great deal longer than touring the whole station, which was understandable. A great deal of paperwork and proofs were required, though luckily there was no need for the standard background checks because she had to get those out of the way just to enter into the academy.

I promise to always use this properly, Serena swore silently as she clipped on her newly registered piece. It hung at her hip, a satisfying weight she remembered from sharpshooting drills at the Academy. *And I promise never to use it at all unless absolutely necessary.*

“Well,” Lieutenant Jacobs said, “I don’t think there’s much more I can do for you here. I’ve got an appointment with the Chief that I have to keep in about half an hour, so let’s go find you someone else to bother.”

They headed back into the land of cubicles, which were all occupied. If there was anything she could say she learned during her 818 hours of training, it was that the war on crime was actually something like 70% paperwork. The unit on proper filing procedures lasted longer than any other single activity.

“Hey, Darcy!” Lieutenant Jacobs barked.

From the corner of the room, a shaggy blonde head lifted up from where it had been almost resting against the computer monitor. The owner of the shaggy hair pushed back from her desk and then spun in her chair to face them both.

Serena gasped. She couldn’t help it.

She always considered herself a straight woman. Whenever she took someone out to the river or by the park to fuck, it had always been a man and it was more or less good. Maybe not as good as she would have liked, but fun enough. She liked to look at men.

But lately, there had been a niggling sense inside her that she might not be fully straight. Bi-curious, was the word for it. People treated that word like it was some temporary disease that college girls caught and then grew out of. Like chicken pox.

She wasn't in college, and she hadn't really had time in the past couple of years to date as much as she wanted so she still wasn't sure whether it was a phase or not. Looking at that cop, though...

Hell, that cop was enough to turn any woman into a lesbian.

It was those eyes. Those emerald eyes. They were so sharp, so keen. They saw right down to your soul in an instant, leaving you bare and exposed to anything she said or did.

And it was the ruffle of her blonde hair, like she'd just come inside and it was all windswept.

It was the way the uniform hugged her body without being promiscuous. Effortless without trying.

It was everything about her, and Serena practically fell in love right then and there.

"Lieutenant," the woman named Darcy said. Her voice carried just the barest trace of warmth, but she wasn't looking at the Lieutenant. She was staring hard at Serena, that sharp gaze so unreadable. "How is your morning?"

"Busy, which is why I've come to drop off our newest rookie with you. Serena, this is Darcy Fairweather. She's the vet in your division, so just think of her as another me and treat her like it."

Darcy cracked a white smile. It hung crooked, roguishly so. Serena felt her lower stomach start to burn with warmth and desire, the way it did when she was undressing a hot guy. "I don't know if that's going to be possible for her. I'm not short enough."

"Ha! Well, she handled herself well enough with our guard Chihuahua at the front desk." Both women rolled their eyes. "But in any case, happy birthday today, Darcy. Serena is your present. Enjoy her."

What does that mean?

"I'm sure I'll find some use for her, Lieutenant," Darcy said. And then they were alone.

Serena peeked at Darcy, suddenly feeling shy. "Hi."

All warm pretenses were dropped the moment she spoke. The veteran looked at her long and hard, that piercing gaze practically splitting her in half in its intensity. Beautiful or not, this woman was going to be quite the force to reckon with. She could feel it.

Chapter Two

"How much did you pass by?"

The little girl standing before her blinked, obviously taken aback by the sudden question. Darcy waited, not moving or blinking. Sure, the woman was grown and at least 21 to have been able to get into the Academy, but compared to Darcy's 30 years, she was nothing more than a baby. A pretty little baby, by the looks of her. She was delicate as hell, whip-thin and dainty-eyed, with a waifish face. Adorable, sure. Enough to get her pussy going, definitely. But cop material?

"I don't really understand," Serena said, looking a little uncomfortable.

Darcy held back a sigh. "Your final exam. How much did you pass by? A few percentage points?"

Realization slowly crossed the other woman's pretty features, and then she furrowed her eyebrows together. The inquisitive look suited her, probably because it matched her clueless personality. "You're implying that I failed?"

"Close. I'm implying that you did slightly better than failing."

"Why do you think that?"

Darcy sat back in her chair and waved her arms, gesturing to Serena. "Because of...this. Kid, you look like a Barbie doll. You look like some pageant girl who hasn't ever lifted anything heavier than a piece of lettuce to your mouth in your whole life. What on earth made you think you can be a cop? What on earth made anyone think you can be a cop? And a beat cop at that. You sure you don't want to head back and reapply for some fancy desk job where you don't have to run around all day?"

She had more to say but just then, Serena held up her hand. The kid looked upset, but not broken down. Surprising, but not very impressive. So she wasn't insecure, but that didn't mean she was going to be worth anything.

"I passed with a 95%. I was in the top ten."

Okay, that was a little bit more impressive. Even Darcy herself hadn't gotten such a high score, though she'd also ended up in the top ten because the Academy just wasn't that impressive when she joined up so long ago. It had barely even been a thing, utterly casual with its students while now it was more like an actual school. Still, that didn't mean much in the long run.

"Okay, Serena. That's pretty good, I'll give you that. But that doesn't mean you have what it takes."

"So I have to prove myself to you now?"

Darcy stood. “That’s exactly it. That’s exactly what you have to do. It’s my job to train you, so I have to see what I’m starting with. Let’s go to the range.”

She headed off down the hall, distinctly aware of the sway of her own hips. She felt energized, almost buzzing. That was just the horniness talking to her, but it felt damn good. It had been awhile since she had anything ahead of her to get excited about, so this was something she figured she could probably enjoy even if she would never allow herself to show it out in the open.

They passed by a detective, who was just exiting the break room with a cup of coffee in one hand. “Hey, Darcy,” the detective said, nodding at her. “Happy birthday. The big three-oh, right?”

The detective, Brian, was pushing forty-five himself. Darcy narrowed her eyes at him. “Maybe someday I’ll be as old as you.”

“Heh, you got a ways to go. But just remember, we got old cops and we got bold cops, but no old bold cops. Be careful out there.”

“I will,” Darcy said. “Hey, have you met my present yet?” She stepped aside to reveal Serena.

Brian nodded. “Saw her when she was getting the tour. Miss, you’re in good hands here so don’t fuck it up.”

“I won’t fuck it up, sir.”

“Sir! Hey! I like this one. She’s polite, unlike you.” Brian clamped his hand on Serena’s shoulder, grinned, and then headed on his way.

Darcy shook her head and sighed. “Anyway, come on.”

She led Serena back out through the station, where they passed by Chad as he dozed at the counter. And then they were outside, the wind mussing her messy hair as they headed over to her cruiser. It was an older model and had seen some better days, if the dented fender and scraped paint were anything to go by, but it had been with her for her whole time on the force. Through chases and oil changes, she knew it in and out. The cruiser was like an extension of her soul, much like a baseball player's beloved bat.

"It's got character," Serena said.

"Sure does," Darcy agreed. Her voice softened. "Been with me through a lot. When it's your time, you'll probably be patrolling around in one of the newer models."

They both piled into the police car. Darcy stroked the steering wheel, and then settled her fingers into the little dimples in the leather which had been worn in with over a decade's worth of gripping. The engine purred for her, resonating so deep within her soul that she very nearly purred back. It was like sliding into a t-shirt and jeans after being on patrol all day, like eating ice cream while watching one of her guilty-pleasure soap operas on TV just before bed. Comfortable.

As they headed out, Darcy glanced sideways at Serena. The kid was sitting upright in the passenger seat, her whole body so tense she was practically bouncing. “Got something up your ass?” she was about to ask, but even just thinking the words conjured up a mental image that she would rather not ponder on too much. Anal was one of her favorite past-times, as she was one of a few lucky women who could cum just from that alone, but it wouldn’t do to think about her new partner like that.

In the end, she didn’t have to say anything because Serena manned up and broke the silence for her. “You said that like it was a bad thing. That I’d be getting to drive a newer model. Why?”

“You’ll think I’m nuts. I’d rather not spend my birthday in a mental hospital, girl.”

“My name is Serena.”

“And you haven’t earned my respect enough yet for me to call you by your name. Kid.” Darcy could have laughed at the indignant look on Serena’s face. She had her attention neatly divided between the road and the younger woman. Luckily by this time of morning, most of the traffic had died down as everyone was already at work. “But I guess if you’re not going to turn me in...”

How to explain this without being a freak?

“I guess it’s the same reason I like flea markets and garage sales. Does that make sense? Maybe not. But new things...Just don’t do it for me. I like something with that character. Something that’s been through the rough and come out with memories. You know if something has made it this long, it’s gonna last you awhile yet.”

Serena murmured, “I see,” and her words practically dripped with awe. A bit of silence fell between them as they drove, but Darcy decided she couldn’t let it stay. Not yet, anyway.

“What are you thinking?”

“I’m thinking that you’re still an ass, but at least you’re a sentimental ass.”

Darcy laughed. “You got me.”

Not too long after that, they pulled up in front of the gun range. Part of the Connecticut Gun Club, it was a favorite of police officers; in fact, 75% of the members of the Club were also on the force. The remainder of that was made up of military folks and the odd handful of enthusiasts.

They checked out some practice pistols and bullets, and headed over to the farthest corner of the range. A target was ready and waiting, and Darcy manipulated the distance so that it was practically a point-blank shot.

“Think you can hit that?”

Serena ignored the words, lined up a shot, and fired off a bullet in less than a second. The bullet landed exactly in the heart, resulting in instant death for their cardboard foe.

Not very impressive. Darcy moved the target back. “How about now?”

Serena glanced at the new distance, readjusted her aim, and fired. Another dead-on shot.

Something was happening, here. Darcy could feel it in her bones. There was something here. The excited, horny buzzing she'd felt before was starting to solidify into something else entirely but she wasn't quite sure of its exact identity yet. A little breathless, she moved the target back again.

Before she'd even finished, Serena fired again. The shot landed dead-center, because of course it did.

Again and again, they repeated the pattern. Each time, Serena fired off a single shot that punctured the cutout's painted heart until it was shredded to bits.

Darcy went to adjust the distance again and found it impossible. It was as far back as it was going to go, and of course Serena nailed the shot like it was no big deal.

"Well, shit," Darcy murmured. "Where the hell did you learn to shoot like that?"

Serena glanced at her. "What do you mean? I'm just going what I was trained to do. Well." She hesitated.

Darcy waved her hand a little. "I know what you mean."

Serena was trained in proper police protocol, which was to shoot to injure and only when absolutely necessary; however, she must have also been trained for perfect accuracy like this before. The ideas were incredibly different and conflicted with one another, as a lot of things did in a cop's life.

"Let's try something else."

"Okay," Serena agreed.

Darcy brought out a new target and positioned it about half of the total distance away. "Fresh clip. Empty it. Fast as you can, as close together as you can. Go."

Before she even gave the word to start, Serena had whipped out a new clip, slammed it into the practice pistol, took aim, and fired eight times in rapid succession. Darcy turned her head quickly to watch as the bullets landed, each one striking the target's skull in a tight little circle. As the seventh bullet hit, she snapped out, "Heart."

And the eighth bullet slammed home in the heart.

"Fuck me sideways. How long have you been shooting?"

Serena relaxed from her shooter's stance, keeping her empty gun pointed in a safe direction. "14 weeks."

Darcy shook her head. Unbelievable. "No way. You had to have gone hunting with your dad before, or something."

"Nope."

"Had a BB gun as a kid?"

"No."

Unbelievable.

Darcy raked her fingers through her hair and shook her head. "Maybe I just don't understand you. Had you ever touched a gun at all before you enrolled in the Academy?"

"No." Serena looked her oddly. "I never have. Bow and arrow in gym class in high school but that was only for a week each year. What's wrong? Didn't I do okay?"

"Serena," Darcy said, using the rookie cop's name, "you just did more than okay. You pretty much just outshot every single person I know."

Delight lit up the young woman's face. "I guess I'm just a natural at this."

"Hell, maybe you are. But what about a moving target?"

Perhaps it would come of no surprise that moving targets were also no problem. This time, Darcy didn't watch the targets. She already knew what was going to happen with that. No, this time she wanted to observe Serena.

"Go," she said.

Serena immediately dropped into the perfect stance, all relaxed angles and firm flexibility. Her arm came up, her finger tightened on the trigger as she took her sight, and then she fired. The gun bucked in her hand, shaking her body and making her breasts bounce around beneath her uniform. She looked so intense and alive, so vibrant, that Darcy couldn't stop herself. Her pussy muscles tensed up so hard it was like a miniature orgasm, watching this adorable women perform so skillfully.

I might actually be in trouble here.

But, she consoled herself, she was a woman of the law. She wouldn't be making any sexual advances on the younger woman. It was a conflict of interest, especially when they were going to be working together directly for a long while.

Although, that probably wasn't going to be as long of a time as she was originally thinking if Serena could perform every aspect of the job with such fervor as she did shooting. Did that make her sad? She couldn't really tell yet.

"You're good," Darcy said. "Real good. A natural for sure."

She meant it, too. And it was obvious that Serena could tell, because that proud glow on her face only intensified. "I'm so glad."

"But," Darcy interrupted, "there's a whole lot more to being a cop than just playing around with guns. I'm going to guess that you learned self-defense."

Serena nodded earnestly.

"Let's go test that out."

Fifteen minutes later and they were at the gym nearby. Hot Stuffs was what Darcy sometimes overheard teenage girls call a "beefcake bar." It was where pretty little gay men and model-type women went to look at all the glistening muscles and hot bodies on display. Typically, treating someone like they belonged in a museum didn't actually result in any sexual encounters –except for the occasional disappointing one, and a handful of love stories. There were no in-betweens- but the guys loved the attention, soaking it up and flirting it out like it was no big deal.

And then there was Darcy. Darcy considered herself the only serious female member of Hot Stuffs. The regulars were her guys. They were her gang, like brothers to her. None of them were cops, so she had no image to uphold around them. She turned a blind eye to the occasional smell of pot, and in return they backed her up whenever a new guy came in and started causing trouble; a few days a month, they all met up at a bar and caused just enough hell to get gently ushered out, but not enough to have the cops called on them.

That would have been awkward.

But, as the kids used to say when she was a kid, this gym was her jam. She loved its off-the-wall nature just as much as she loved her cruiser and her job.

Serena laughed when she saw where they were going, though. “Seriously? Here? I thought this place was for prostitutes.”

“I guess prostitutes have to work out sometime, too,” Darcy joked. She had to admit, this day was a lot more fun than she thought it was going to be.

They stepped through the front double doors and entered an entirely new world composed of sweat, steam, and the musky scent of rampant testosterone. One of the workers who was standing in the lobby and unashamedly flirting with a guy fresh out of the shower, turned and noticed them. He was a handsome little guy, a little stereotypical and a little too fussy, but a good person all the same.

His round face lit up. “Hey, Darcy!” he called, trilling her name on the second syllable. “Like, wow! It’s been ages!”

“It’s been four days,” she replied teasingly, smiling at him. She couldn’t help it. For all his appearance, he was a serial heartbreaker; he was a little twink of a gay man, drawing in the big scary bears like nobody's business before dropping them and moving onto the next. "Is Petie here today?"

"Sure is! You know it. He's teaching a class right now but like, it's almost over. You can head back right now and probably just catch him on his way out."

"Thanks, sweetie," she said, and passed on through the lobby. She knew every single guy in the room, most of the rubberneckers who were just there for the show, and she greeted all of them as she passed.

From behind here, she heard Serena mutter, "Of all the people I could be partnered up with..."

They left the lobby and entered a back hallway which was slightly less crowded. Several courts and doorways branched off of the hall, leading to locker areas, showers, play areas, and a storage room. Darcy paused for a moment, figuring that she owed the rookie a bit of an explanation. Hard to pinpoint why she felt that way, except she knew it had to do with the fact that this girl was earning her respect at a startling rate.

“You’re with me because I train the new officers. It’s what I do.”

“But you’re just a regular cop, right? You don’t have a fancy name or title or anything.”

Darcy looked into Serena’s eyes. They were warm and brown, so utterly sweet she had to restrain herself from devouring her right then and there. “Thanks,” she teased, and then continued to talk over the young woman’s embarrassed protestations. “You know, it’s true that I’m just a regular cop. I didn’t specialize. But I did that on purpose. About 5 years after I joined up, I started looking around to see if there was anything specific I wanted to move towards, but once you start heading up the ladder things get real specific. I get bored too easy for that, so I just stuck around.

“I’ve trained fifteen rookies like you. 1 is dead. 4 left the state. Another two joined the Army after deciding this wasn’t grand enough for them. 6 moved on to specialize here at the department. Another just left the force because he got injured and decided he still wanted to be alive to see his daughter get born.”

"That's only fourteen."

"I don't count Chad." Darcy grimaced. "He was the last one I trained. Idiot. Small and yappy. There's a reason we call him the Chihuahua. After him, I requested for Lieutenant Jacobs to give me a fucking break but I guess she decided my break was over when you joined us."

Memories flooded through her as she spoke to Serena of all the people she'd trained. She loved and hated all of them in varying ways, and there were some who just stuck out in her mind more than the others whether that was for better or worse. Chad was certainly one. She'd been pretty fond of those Army kids, though they had been even more idyllic and innocent than this girl. And Hannah...

Her heart broke just a little bit. Her first rookie. Her first serious love.

"Darcy?"

She shook her head to clear away the mental fog. The past was the past, and she'd gotten over that months ago. "Sorry. Us old people like to just wander down memory lane sometimes. Let's go find Petie."

Petie was a self-defense expert, a black belt and judo master, a yoga instructor, and many other things. If it required an able body to do it, Petie knew how it was done.

For the next half an hour, she stood on the sidelines and watched as Serena threw Petie around the padded self-defense classroom. She had requested that he not hold himself back, and judging by how heavily he was breathing he had taken her seriously; because of her small size, Serena had to find other ways to compensate when it came to fighting. The Police Academy should have taught her all about that, and it looked like it had. She was a tricky, wily little fish of a fighter, dancing all over the place and using every bit of momentum she had to her advantage.

Finally, Petie called a stop to the session. Serena relaxed, her chest heaving as she breathed hard. Forcing herself not to look at it, Darcy addressed her friend, "So?"

"She's damn good," Petie huffed.

I really am in some trouble here, she thought, a little bit amazed. "Alright, I guess we can head out on an actual patrol now."

No matter how hard she tried to sound neutral, she just couldn't hide the little bit of warmth that had somehow found its way into her voice. She reserved that for people she actually liked, but apparently she didn't have a choice in the matter this time.

Chapter Three

As is the way of things, the next couple of weeks flew by. The life of a police officer was rarely relaxed and always varied, even if that variation was just in the schedule. Serena had one day off a week, and she would work 8 to 12 hours in a day, and her day off was never set in stone. As it turned out, Darcy also liked to pick up extra time and she often called on Serena to accompany her.

It wasn't all as bad as it seemed, however. Serena really had nothing else going on in her life to drag at her, and she found that she would rather be spending time learning the ropes with the older cop rather than staying at home. Even on her days off, she found that she really didn't enjoy the break. She hadn't become a cop to take breaks.

Or maybe it was simply the fact that she missed Darcy when they were apart.

The first few days were fairly average. Serena knew for her whole life that Hartford was incredibly dangerous for a city of its size. She wasn't quite sure what the reason for it was, but people living in Hartford made only half as much money as people who commuted here to work. That meant there was a lot of thievery and assaults which targeted outside workers.

Their job was to patrol the city on a set schedule that changed every day on a rotation, paying close attention to high-risk areas. Of course, that means both the high-end places and the areas where buildings were sinking into the dirt they were so poorly maintained.

“I live in a place kind of like this,” Serena said, pointing out the window at a trailer park neighborhood during one of their first ever patrols together. The quality of the trailers themselves might have been okay once upon a time but the area had clearly fallen into a state of disrepair. There were pipes exposed all over the place, boarded-up windows, and the grass was so tall it was practically a jungle.

Darcy glanced at her with a bit of a pained expression on her face. “I thought you told me that your truck’s locks don’t work.”

She nodded. “Right. They don’t.”

Darcy heaved a huge sigh. "You are incredibly lucky that no one has ever broken into it when you're sleeping."

"I guess I am. But hopefully I'll make enough money soon that I can buy a new truck."

"In your dreams. Cops don't get paid that much."

"I know," Serena snorted. "That doesn't really seem fair to me. But, you forget that this is kind of my first real job."

"Hmm." Darcy stopped at a red sign, and then took a left to circle back around the neighborhood in the opposite direction. While this wasn't exactly a high-alert place where they had to keep their guard up, they'd been getting in some anonymous tips and rumors that a drug trade might be occurring here, or else passing through the area. One might think that a person selling drugs would know how to hide their stuff, but that wasn't always the case. It's hard to be crafty when you're high off your rocker and hallucinating. Plus, some people didn't seem to understand that you had to come into the trade with connections already made. Darcy already told Serena of the time that she came across a perfectly normal guy who was carrying around flyers advertising how pure the heroin was that he was selling. He had even included business hours and an address. She just showed up during his hours and arrested him.

The best part, she said, was that he looked absolutely baffled about how she'd managed to find him so easily.

Remembering that made her laugh. It was a good sound, just deep enough to be sexy without venturing into throaty.

"So, what was your first job, then?"

"Fast food."

"Oh god."

"I know," she agreed. "It's pretty awful. But I just didn't want to be home anymore and I wasn't old enough to go into the Academy yet, so I had to go something. But I didn't want to get into something that wasn't going to be more of a drain on my money than it was a help, you know?"

"Which makes both of us uneducated pansies," Darcy said, and pulled away from the neighborhood. "But you do what you have to do."

"Yes," Serena murmured. "You do."

She could tell that Darcy wanted to pry and figure out exactly what that meant, and she would have told her right then and there after only knowing her for less than a week at that point, but the older cop didn't push it. The conversation turned to safer things, like work, and co-workers, and observations of the lives going on around them.

Most of the time though, they just drove in silence together except for what absolutely needed saying.

What Serena quickly gained proof of was something that she had been certain of for quite a long time, from hearing her older brother talk about it and just from common sense: the life of a cop wasn't stable for very long. Those first few days were lucky, letting her get a grip on the flow of things before throwing her a curveball.

But a curveball it was, because on her fourth day on the job, a call came in over their radio.

"Any cruisers near 48 Washington?" came the query, static clinging to every syllable.

Serena tensed up immediately because they had actually just passed by Washington Avenue in their patrol and hadn't seen anything wrong. All it took was one second for disaster to strike, though.

Darcy glanced over at her, and she suddenly remembered that as the co-pilot, she was supposed to be the one handling the radio. She reached out for it but was too slow. The veteran threw the cruiser over onto the shoulder of the road without even slowing down, making cars in the lane she passed over honk and squeal on their brakes, until they saw that it was a police car. And then there was nothing but orderly silence as the drivers adjusted themselves, and the city-goers cruising down the sidewalk suddenly found more interesting things to worry about and hurried on their way.

Grabbing the mouthpiece, Darcy brought it near her face. "This is Cruiser 99," she boomed out, her voice taking on a commanding presence which Serena had never heard from her before. This gorgeous woman was obviously multi-faceted and she kept discovering new aspects of her all the time. "We're right nearby. What's going on?"

"Got a call over 911," the other voice said over the radio. The voice was calm and measured, but hurried in a professional sort of manner. This was a person used to getting things done in a tense situation. Before the speaker could even continue, Darcy was already flipping on their lights, siren, and burning rubber streaks across the street as she spun into a crazy U-turn back the way they'd come. "Wasn't very clear. Someone saying something about a gun. A male voice spoke to the caller, and the caller hung up without another word. 911 called back, no answer."

"Got it," Darcy snapped, spitting out the words like watermelon seeds. "We're already there."

Isn't this kind of a time for stealth? Serena wondered. If something was going on, the sirens would have put an end to it the second they came on. Their perps would dive back into the rat holes they'd emerged from.

Once again, she was a little bit slow on the uptake. They were already almost there and she was still sitting relaxed in the front seat like a little kid in mom's minivan heading for ice cream after a dentist appointment. Going bolt-upright, she reached down to fumble with her piece around the seatbelt.

Darcy's hand whipped out. "Don't," she said. "Not until I tell you. Stay in the cruiser. The word is lemon."

Her heart beating nearly as fast as the other woman was driving, Serena nodded rapidly.

"Actually, can you scrunch down? Just so no one can look in the window and see you? Do it, we're here."

Serena undid her seatbelt, wasting precious seconds by fumbling with the buckle before she was able to slither down into the empty footspace. It was incredibly cramped but she just about managed it because of her smile size.

There was shouting as they whipped around the corner at 70 mph, and then Darcy slammed on the brakes and leapt out of the car before it had even come to a full stop. She could feel it still lightly rolling away beneath her tangled legs. Holding her breath, she tried to piece together the scene without being able to see it at all.

"Police Department! Everyone stop!"

There wasn't even a bit of air, only the sound of Serena's pulse throbbing in her ears. No one moved or spoke, like the whole world obeyed Darcy's command. She imagined the veteran standing there in the middle of a nearby overgrown yard, her uniform stretched taut in all the right –or wrong- places so that the curves of her muscles bulged threateningly. And there would be other curves straining against her clothes as well.

Serena swallowed hard, struggling to get herself focused back on what was at hand. A standoff of some kind. She really shouldn't be thinking so sexually. She shouldn't be thinking sexually at all!

Then, someone spoke and it definitely wasn't Darcy.

"Back off, pig dyke. This got nothin' to do wit' you."

Darcy spoke again immediately, her voice accompanied by a tiny metallic clicking sound as she shifted her pistol around a little for added effect. "It's got everything to do with me, kid. This is my job. Since you seem to want to be the one to speak for everyone else, why don't you tell me what was going on here when I pulled up?"

Serena practically heard the kid scowl. She mentally readjusted her perceptions. This wasn't some gang turf thing. This was some teenager with a revenge complex, probably.

"Ain't none of your business, bitch." There was a far less calculated mechanical rattle. A different caliber. She tensed.

The kid was getting ready. He was going to shoot at any second! Why wasn't Darcy saying anything?

"Pretty sure you don't want to do that, son."

Serena stopped. Darcy's voice changed. It was more mellow now, almost soothing in tone. And she'd switched from calling the guy "kid" to addressing him as the more personal "son." It was a textbook tactic but Serena was scared it was only going to serve to make the kid more mad than he already was.

But that was the exact opposite of what happened. "You right. I ain't wanting to."

There was another click. She had to force herself to stay hidden. She was dying to look. As it was, she was about to get her wish.

"You fucking pansy shit, I'll do it!"

"Lemon," Darcy said so calmly that Serena almost missed it. But her body reacted before her brain could register and she leapt up, throwing herself out of the car and coming up in a roll again with her gun traveling around wildly to try and find the target to nail while also struggling to assess the situation.

There was a small gathering of teenagers, only a few years younger than Serena herself. Most of them were young men, though she saw a chick or two in the mix. There was a smaller, scrawnier body with a gun in hand, pointing at the ground, and then there was a larger guy who looked like he might be on the football team. He had his gun shoved up against the head of an elderly woman, who looked so terrified she was practically already dead.

Serena finally settled her gun on him, her heart pounding. But now that she was here, now that she was in the moment, she found that she could speak. What she said was, “Freeze.”

And Darcy snorted.

The football jock scowled at them. “What, you had your little girlfriend tucked away in the back of your shitty car? That where you fuck her?”

"At least I got a lady to fuck," Darcy said. She looked absolutely unfazed, while Serena felt like she was about to explode just from the pressure of her heart alone. "Unlike you, chickenshit."

The childish insult seemed to surprise him. "What the hell you call me?"

"Hey, Johnny," the smaller boy said weakly, but a quick look from everyone else shut him up fast.

"I called you a chickenshit. I can call you a lot of other things too if that's the way you wanna do things." Darcy's voice had changed again, rising and falling in the same cadence with which the teenagers spoke to her; rough and uncultured, it spoke of kids with parents who worked too hard, too late, who were never home. It spoke of a home that wasn't a very good place to be anyway. "Speaking of calling, we got at least one other police cruiser full of bored pigs comin' this way. Maybe two or three, depending on how many bored extras we had sittin' around in traffic. You're going to be outnumbered and riddled full of holes if you don't start telling me what the fuck you guys are doing."

The football jock, who seemed to be named Johnny, opened his mouth to speak.

Darcy cut her eyes across at Serena, a barely perceptible motion that she had been waiting for this whole time. At the cue, Serena moved her gun in a very dramatic manner. The jock screamed like a little girl, and then clamped his hands over his mouth.

The girls in the group giggled at him, pointing and laughing.

"Only he gets to talk," Darcy said, gesturing at the smaller boy.

He'll break easier.

He was already broken. That scowl never left his face but he was broken. "Johnny's tryin' to join the X's. They said he had to kill someone. And then they said he had to talk someone else into killing for him 'cause they're trying to be more clever. He picked me. He told me he'd get me in, too. And he had to do it in front of enough witnesses."

Just then, there was a wail of approaching sirens.

The next several hours were practically insane. Arrests were made, parents were called, kids were shuttled around...

The smaller guy was let off the hook, though he would going to be sent back to an alternative school for the third time, while the football player was due to stand trial for attempted murder.

When it was all said and done and she had been dismissed, Serena started to head outside when a hand on her arm stopped her.

Turning, she saw it was none other than Darcy. “I’m going to bet no one told you this yet but you did pretty good out there.”

“It was intense,” Serena said.

“You changing your mind about all this?”

"I can't."

"I didn't think so." Darcy took a step back, leaning one full hip against the wall as she spoke. "You know, I wouldn't have pulled any of that fancy signal shit around a newcomer if it was anyone but you."

"That means a lot to me," Serena said truthfully.

"But my trust in you comes with a price." Darcy fixed her with a firm look. "You got something up your sleeve and I need to know what it is."

"It's pretty personal," she began, but Darcy really didn't seem to care. "Okay. My brother used to be a cop. Used to. He got killed on the job."

"Your last name is Blake, right? I remember your brother. He was going into detective training, right? Not in my circle but he seemed like a good enough kid. I'm so sorry."

She shrugged. The pain of his loss was dulled with the years since then, but she knew it would never entirely leave her. “Thank you. But that’s really what set me on this path, you know? I never want any family to have to go through what mine did.”

“That’s a pretty damn idyllic way of looking at things. No offense,” Darcy said. “But....you know, I understand. It’s equal parts anger and sadness. The first rookie I ever trained...my partner...”

“I’m sorry,” Serena said now, and she was, but her thoughts were also full of questions as she examined the choice of words more than the situation called for. Partner. Romantic? Or a work relationship?

“Hey, you want to go get a drink with me?”

“I really do,” she said. This was all getting way too much out of hand for her.

Chapter Four

After that eventful first weeks, the routine was truly established: patrolling with the occasional burst of excitement. Nothing ever turned out to be quite as severe as the standoff with the would-be gang members but there were drunk drivers to apprehend and the occasional marijuana bust. Nothing too difficult, although Serena felt that just by being around Darcy, her head was being crammed full of knowledge.

This wasn't one of those times, however. It was nearing the very end of their patrol together and they were circling back through some of the more risky areas before returning to the station. Darcy seemed unusually quiet, quieter than she normally was, and that gave her a bad sort of feeling.

"Hey," Serena said, trying to encourage her to talk.

"What is it?"

"Is everything okay? Are you having a problem with...anything?" She didn't exactly know how to phrase the question. During her brief time in the force, it had come to her attention that Darcy was a complete and utter lesbian. It wasn't anything really in the way she acted around other women, though Serena only saw her around civilians while working or near the other female cops. Maybe it was a bit in the way she acted around men, and the way men treated her, but that could also simply have been a sign that she was just a tomboy and had earned their respect the hard way.

The reality was in the subtle clues in what was said to her teasingly, and the remarks she made in return. She understood a bit better now all the jokes that had been made about Serena being her present. No one took it seriously, and as Darcy's birthday faded into the past, the jokes slowly faded away until they were gone entirely. Until that happened though, she collected just enough clues to figure out that the rookie she lost had definitely been a romantic interest, and that she had been a dainty woman.

Basically, Serena was exactly Darcy's type. The cop hadn't done anything to hit on her, and she didn't think the occasional night out at the bar together really counted as a date. That was something friends did, especially when people from that weird gym kept wandering in and out all the time to interrupt them. Plus, a bar wasn't exactly the most romantic place in the world.

So why am I a little disappointed that she doesn't want to date me?

That would be a conflict of interest, anyway.

"I was just thinking about how far you've come since your first real day."

The concealed praise made her soul glow a little, but then she paused. “Why does that sound like a goodbye? Are you skipping out on me?”

“Nah,” Darcy said, and scanned the darkened road in front of them before steering the cruiser in the direction of the station. “Don’t worry about that. Only the good die young so I’m going to be here forever, basically.”

She flinched a little. “Hey, who mentioned death?”

“I’m tired as death,” Darcy joked, and that was all.

The next day, Serena hurried into the building in a rush and scanned the room for a sign of the older woman. Nothing.

Chad waved at her from behind the counter. “Hey, fresh meat,” he said, as he always did. At least that was the same.

And then Darcy emerged from the hallway leading to the offices, and Serena let out a breath she hadn’t known she was holding. Everything was right with the world.

“Hi,” she said.

Darcy greeted her. “Hey.” There were dark circles beneath her eyes, making her look like she hadn’t gotten much sleep. “Ready to head out today?”

“Sure,” she agreed, because there was really no other option, and then she followed her partner out into the parking lot. Darcy’s shoulders sagged, and she really looked exhausted.

It’s not safe to let her drive like this.

As they reached the cruiser, Serena reached out and stopped her with a hand over hers. The touch startled her. The first time they had ever touched, and she had initiated it so eagerly they were practically holding hands; a flush of warmth began to burn up from her fingertips, traveling the length of her wrist and all the way up her arm, across her shoulder, and into her heart. From there, the warmth warped and concentrated into trickling fire. Something ignited deep within her. Something very hot and inexplicable.

Darcy's mouth opened slightly. Serena couldn't look away from those luscious lips, at the tiny hint of pink tongue hidden within. She tried, but all she managed to do was look up and their gazes locked.

She felt exactly like she had all those times when the job got intense, but now it was a thousand times worse somehow.

The intensity was awful, and she could hardly manage to remember why she'd done this in the first place.
"So...uh...Yeah...Let me drive today."

Darcy kept staring at her, making her worried that she hadn't managed to really speak English. "Excuse me?"

"Why don't you let me drive today?" she insisted. "I...I know the patrols and everything. I know where to go, and you look like you could use a break. I know it can't be easy to deal with me like this all the time."

Her half-hearted attempt at a self-deprecating joke went unnoticed. "Thanks for the offer but I'm fine. Just a little tired."

"Sure, I understand. But I still wish you'd let me do it. I need to learn sometime, don't I?"

Apparently her partner was more exhausted than she even thought, because she just sighed and shook her head. "Fine. Thanks."

They piled into the cruiser and headed out. Serena had never been a fan of driving with passengers in her vehicle, because she liked to focus on what she was doing instead of on anyone else who might be there in the way of her concentration, but Darcy stayed quiet as they navigated out through the busy main roads before heading off to one of the smaller suburbs.

The blonde cop had her eyes closed and her face turned toward the window, her breathing slow and thoughtful. *Probably asleep,* Serena thought. That was fine with her. She needed it.

She settled into the drive. After an hour however, Darcy started to stir. "What?" she muttered, and rubbed her eyes on the back of her hands like a child waking from a nap.

"It's okay," Serena said softly. "Just me."

"Uh...Bailey? No..." Darcy shook her head and sat up straighter, looking around. Serena said nothing as she got her bearings, waiting for her to be the first one to talk. "How long was I out?"

"Not very long. You can do it again if you like."

"No. I'm fine for now, thank you." Judging by the shadows beneath her eyes still, that wasn't the case. But she didn't push it, sensing there was more to come. "I really do mean that. Thank you for this. I haven't been sleeping well lately."

"Does it have anything to do with that name? Bailey?"

Darcy sighed and looked down at her hands. "Yes. She was...She was the partner I lost. The rookie I told you about when you first joined up." She sighed. "This is the week of the anniversary of her death. She was in a coma for a few days before...before she went, so this week always fucks me up."

There seemed to be something else hidden within those words, a portent of things to come, but if there were Serena couldn't figure out what they might mean for her and the other cop. If anything. She kept getting ahead of herself like that.

I'm not even ahead of myself, though. I'm way out to the side in la-la land where things like this can actually happen to people like me. As if. Besides, I'm not even sure I like women.

But she could tell herself that all she wanted. That didn't make it true.

Darcy dozed in and out for the rest of the patrol, and then they went their separate ways. The day after that was Serena's day off, and she spent most of it puttering around her apartment pretending to clean and really thinking about the heartthrob lesbian. She was undoubtedly a heartthrob. And a pussy-throb, come to think of it.

Serena came back into work feeling just as tired as Darcy looked two days before, and started to look around for her.

“Hey, rookie,” a voice said. She turned to see Lieutenant Jacobs approaching her, looking even warmer than she had that very first day.

“Hi,” Serena said. “I was just looking for Darcy.”

“Don’t bother,” the Lieutenant said, and beamed. “Have I got a surprise for you! Come on out to the parking lot with me, okay?”

I really hope this isn’t what I think it is.

It was.

Jacobs led her around to the side of the building where the parking lot continued to wrap around. There were cruisers and personal vehicles everywhere of course, and she followed her superior over to one in particular. It was a clean little thing with a modern interpretation of the design, all white with stark accents.

The Lieutenant stood there for a moment, just beaming at her, but when it became obvious that she wasn't going to say anything, she said, "Congratulations, rookie! You're officially on your own from here on out. This baby belongs to you."

"On my own?" Serena repeated. Her heart gave a little twinge. No more long quiet periods spent in good company? No more working together or speculative conversations. No more Darcy. "Are you...are you sure about that?"

Jacobs seemed a little disappointed that her news wasn't being taken with the enthusiasm that she expected, but she didn't comment on it. "Well, for you, I would have liked to keep you where you are for as long as I could, but that just isn't possible"

What does that mean?

"Any other rookie would still have a few months of this ahead of them, but you're too good for that and everyone has noticed. If I kept you where you are needlessly, they'd know what I've got up my sleeve. But I don't like to do that to people, put them on the spot like that."

"I'm...I'm afraid I don't really understand what you mean."

"Well, just between you and me, your position puts you in risk of having a conflict of interest. I wish I could keep you two together like this but I can't. So, this is both a good promotion and bad one, if you understand me."

"I still don't," Serena said, but deep in the back of her mind, she did. The Lieutenant was trying to set her up with Darcy.

"Hmm," was all that Jacobs said on the matter. "Well anyway, I need you to pick up the information on your new route and then get to it. Remember that you both earned this, and it's also a special privilege. Stay within the lines and don't cause any trouble, okay?"

“I definitely will, and I definitely won’t,” she promised.

The Lieutenant gave her the information on the new route, and Serena walked back out to her brand new cruiser with the papers in hand, while fielding congratulations from the other officers. If she was judging the timing of all this correctly, her route would overlap in several areas with the path Darcy always took, though they would never quite meet. Something about that saddened her. She would just have to hope they were above to meet up outside of work at the bar a few times a week to catch up, or something.

Heck, maybe she’d join her gym. It would be worth it just to see her, maybe catch a glimpse of her glistening-wet in the shower...

“Serena,” Darcy said.

Serena had been climbing into her new cruiser. Surprised, she jumped up and managed to firmly whack the top of her head on the underside of the roof. “Fuck,” she said, and rubbed her head while backing out and looking at the woman she had come to consider a friend. “Hey, I guess you heard the news then?”

“I did. Congratulations. I’ll miss you.”

Those three words were enough to knock her off her feet, and she leaned back hard against the car. “I...uh...I’ll miss you, too. I really will.”

“I can tell.” Darcy flashed a mischievous grin. “I have to say, this is the first time I’ve ever swept someone off their feet without even touching them.”

Serena just had to smile back. That grin was just too handsome to ignore. Darcy was handsome. Handsome and beautiful, with the sunlight in her hair and her hands on her proud hips.

Where do we go from here?

She didn’t even have to ask the question out loud. Darcy pulled out a cell phone from her pocket and turned it on. “Since you and I aren't going to be able to cruise around anymore, I'll give you my number. I'd hate to fall out of touch with someone like you."

Serena agreed. They exchanged numbers and then just stood there, both of them with words on the tips of their tongues and not quite knowing how to get them out. Their gazes locked again, like they had when Serena touched Darcy's hand, and she felt the same slow spread of warmth throughout her whole body; the heat was so intense she actually spared a moment to wonder how well she could drive while masturbating, and then scolded herself.

"I guess I should let you go," Darcy finally said. "Good luck out there. Text me all about it sometime tonight, won't you?"

That was exactly what she did. Every minute of the day after that was spent in breathless waiting, just so she could text Darcy from beneath the covers that night, struggling to remember a single moment of it to talk about.

Chapter Five

Relying on the police officer's logic, Serena waited patiently for her luck to change. She expected those first few patrols to turn into disasters, but the population of Hartford seemed to have decided to be unanimously respectful of police officers for the weekend. But trouble follows calm, and one morning not long after she'd started out, there came a call over her radio.

"Any officers near Pixie's?"

Pixie's was a shady bar favored by drug dealers and questionable businessmen, and hardly more than a strip club with the level of undress required for the servers. Serena had never been inside but Darcy made sure to describe every business they ever passed in great detail so she would be prepared.

A quick glance at the GPS confirmed her suspicions, and she reached over to grab the mouthpiece and brought it near her nervous lips. “This is cruiser 119, reporting. Pixie’s is just around the corner from my location. What’s the situation?”

She wished she could sound like Darcy when she said all that, so confident and mature, but instead her voice shook and her hands were trembling so badly that she very nearly dropped the mouthpiece.

“Got a call from the owner. Some guy in a leather jacket got a bit too drunk, hit on one of the servers, and then beat up one of the other patrons when they tried to intervene. Got an ambulance headed out to take care of that, but the drunk perp got in his car and is headed out. Got some more calls in immediately. He’s not in any condition to be out there.”

“Got it,” Serena confirmed, and turned on her lights, and then flipped the switch to start blaring her sirens. The sound was muffled on the inside of the vehicle, but so loud still that she couldn’t hear what the dispatcher said in response. All she could do was hope that it was a confirmation, because she was using all her concentration to focus on the road. She couldn't have replied even if she wanted to, and she certainly couldn't even bother to hang up the damn mouthpiece. It dangled on the cord, clunking around and thumping her thigh as she drove.

As she shot past Pixie's bar, it occurred to her that she maybe should have stayed on line with the dispatcher because she had no idea what direction the drunk driver was headed in. Luckily, that dilemma solved itself in the form of distant honking. How she managed to hear it through her siren was a miracle, but hear it she did. Swerving a sharp right down an alley which she confirmed existed through a split-second glance at her GPS, she shoved her foot down so that the gas pedal touched the floor of the cruiser. The vehicle, which she was only just beginning to know well, jerked forward and the speedometer hit places she never knew existed until now.

Her eyes desperately scanned the scene before her, flicking around rapidly to try and make sense of all the objects which flew by seemingly faster than light. Everything was a blur as she left the alley and cut across a strip of grass to rejoin the highway. She reacted on pure instinct, her thoughts left too far behind to rely on. Faces, other vehicles, lights –none of it mattered as she sank deep into that fevered zone.

There.

Ahead of her, rapidly appearing in the distance, a blue Mustang wove drunkenly in and out of traffic. The wheels practically wobbled as the vehicle shambled around under the inexpert control of the driver. The pace was nowhere near as fast as she had expected, and she slammed her foot down on the brakes in surprise. Her neck snapped forward so hard that she very nearly knocked herself out on the steering wheel, but she recovered well enough –so she thought- and slid quickly into the stream of other cars with only a few inches to spare from the front bumper of the approaching vehicle. Even with her siren and lights blaring, the other driver seemed startled and very nearly caused a wreck behind her. She saw a split glimpse in the rearview mirror, enough to know that a crisis had been just barely avoided, and then the sight slid away as she put on more speed again to catch up to the drunk driver.

The driver had obviously noticed her at this point. He –or she- began to rapidly speed up, cutting in front of other cars.

Meanwhile, as the rest of the drivers on the road caught on to what was happening, they started to part around her cruiser like a biblical sea. Encouraged, she jammed her foot on the gas again and started to catch up. Mustangs were built for speed however, and the progress gained was too small. Her heart hammered in her throat with the adrenaline of the chase and she knew she would have to make her move quickly or risk this stretch of luck running out; if any injuries occurred because of this chase, because of her, she would probably land a position behind the counter that Chihuahua Chad only just managed to escape.

How would Darcy do it?

The question flashed through her mind.

Swerving to the left to blast around a truck that was pulling out of the way too slowly, Serena threw her hand out and snatched at the mouthpiece. A flip of a switch and a rapid button-press later, she shouted into the speaker, "This is the Hartford Police. Pull over now."

The voice that came out of the speaker was unintelligible but commanding and fierce. No one would have been able to understand it anyway beneath the siren, which was exactly why she did it.

The driver seemed to hesitate, faltering behind the wheel for a split second before speeding up again.

"Pull over!" she demanded again, but nothing happened. The driver must have had their foot all the way down on the gas now, which meant there was only one thing left for her to do and nowhere else to go.

She gave the gas everything she had, felt that magical jump again as the cruiser automatically shifted gears, and then shot forward. She swished past the Mustang, and then almost immediately she cut her speed. Not entirely. By only a fraction. But it was enough. The Mustang had to slow down.

And she kept dropping her speed, faster and faster, swerving into the other lane whenever the Mustang tried to get around her. This was a maneuver which she practiced along with all the other rookies at the Academy, but at a sedate pace of 20 mph. Any other cop would have scorned her solo attempt now because this maneuver typically called for two vehicles at least; however, she had taken a risk in banking on the fact that the driver would be too drunk to try backtracking. And it worked, as she dropped down to an even lower speed. Finally turning off her siren, but keeping her lights, she spoke into the mouthpiece again. Her voice was hoarse from the screaming she'd been doing, hoarse from adrenaline, hoarse from how she was tightening her throat to keep from trembling, and it made her sound gruff and not at all small and delicate.

"You have been caught. Stop your vehicle and step out with your hands in the air."

She didn't quite expect it to work, but it did. The Mustang halted entirely, and she stepped on her own brakes to bring the cruiser to a stop, too. The driver's side door of the car behind her opened, and she quickly flipped from the speaker to the radio. "Dispatch, this is cruiser 119. Perp is being detained as we speak."

Without waiting for a reply, she stepped out of the vehicle and went to go make acquaintances with the drunken man who was leaning over with his hands stuck straight out and a puddle of bile forming at his feet.

“Sir,” she said, “you are under arrest.”

Chapter Six

“Hey, Fairweather.”

Darcy glanced up from her paperwork, swishing a few stray hairs off of her forehead with one hand while the other kept a tight hold on her traveling pen. Paperwork. So much paperwork. It seemed like there was no job in the world which involved more paperwork than being a police officer. Normally she would have been glad for the break, would have relished the chance to talk to another human being instead of staring at the same sheets of paper over and over again every week, but this time she was just annoyed.

Ever since Serena got her own cruiser and their patrols were separate, she'd been feeling incredibly out of sorts. Well, perhaps it had started before that. The week before this was simply awful, as she mourned Bailey's loss anew. She suspected it was the same sort of grief that Serena felt on the anniversary of her brother's death, but she also suspected it wasn't quite the same. Hers was sharper, not so dulled with time. Not dulled at all. A lack of sleep combined with not taking proper care of her health meant she was already bent out of sorts, and now she didn't even have the patrols with that silly rookie to look forward to.

Except, she was far from silly.

"Lieutenant," Darcy said casually. Even though she respected her superior and knew that she herself had a flawless record, her heart still skipped a beat every time she was spoken to by this powerful woman. She imagined it was much the same way that normal citizens felt when a cop spoke to them, like their every movement was being judged intensely and without remorse. "Can I help you with something?"

"I actually wanted to congratulate you." Lieutenant Jacobs grinned broadly and then spread her hands happily. "So, congratulations."

"Well, thank you," Darcy said drily, "but I don't know what you're congratulating me for. As far as I'm aware, I haven't done anything very spectacular lately."

"Not directly, but you're certainly a factor. Even if you aren't, I'm going to say that you are. Your protégé made her first solo arrest today."

Serena made her first arrest. Already. I knew she had it in her.

Yes. Serena, who was far from silly. Serena, who was fantastic in her own right. Serena, who she could not deny that she now had a crush on. It was inevitable, and now it was a reality. It had been a long time since Darcy actually drooled after a woman like this. Ever since Bailey died, she had kept herself supplied with the occasional monthly foray into sex just for the release and to keep her skills –and she was skilled, indeed- but actual emotional attachment had been nil. She went into a bar, picked up a tipsy woman who wasn't slobbering drunk, and they had their fun before parting ways; her tastes ran in the range of small and delicate, girls who would let her take the wheel and guide the act. Serena certainly fit the mold, but this was more than simple physical attraction.

Bringing herself back to the conversation, Darcy said, "I guess that's some good news. Mind if I ask what exactly she got herself into for that to happen?"

"Why don't you ask her yourself when she gets back to pick up the paperwork before heading home?" Lieutenant Jacobs asked, her eyes glowing. "In fact, why don't you head home an hour early tonight?"

That would mean she got off at the same time as Darcy. She raised an eyebrow. "Lieutenant, you wouldn't happen to be trying to set me up, would you?"

"No," she said, drawing out the single syllable much too long for it to actually be true. "I just think there's a time-honored tradition of vets buying the rookies a drink when they hit their first big-boy milestone, and you two would look very nice sitting at a table together."

"Get out of here," Darcy said shortly, and she walked away laughing.

Despite her outward irritation, she could help but to feel a little thrill of genuine excitement. This might be her chance. A chance for what was something she wasn't entirely certain of, but it would be a chance all the same.

It was very hard to concentrate on reading after that, so she left the paperwork for another time and went out on an early patrol. Of course, she timed her arrival so that she was pulling in just at the same time as Serena.

The young woman saw her and her whole tired face seemed to light up with a glow like never before. Her mouth moved, saying her name. The sight of her, so happy, made Darcy happy, too.

They met up outside the front of the building. Serena looked exhausted and stressed out, as limp as a used dish rag, but there was still that glow about her even so close up.

“Hey, Se...” Darcy started to say, and then stopped in surprise as a pair of strong arms wrapped around her midsection. The other’s warm body pressed against hers, long hair escaping from that tight bun to tickle her neck. Her scent was sweat, adrenaline, and the last remnants of a floral perfume. After a moment, she held her back and breathed in deeply. Everything about this was so strange and yet so familiar that she wanted to sink into the embrace, yet had to hold herself back.

Just a little longer, she thought, not quite sure yet what she was waiting for.

“I was so scared,” the younger woman muttered against her neck. Her breath was hot, and started something fiery stirring around in her lower midsection.

This is what I'm waiting for. Alright then.

No matter what her mind or heart said, her body had spoken first.

Darcy pulled back a little, but didn't entirely leave the embrace; not only did she not want to, she also suspected that Serena needed it to continue for a little longer yet. "I heard you had some fun today but no one told me exactly what happened," she said. "Do you maybe want to head out and get a drink with me to talk about it?"

Serena nodded. "I need to pick up the paperwork and then I'll be right back."

Once she returned, Darcy reached out and placed a hand on her arm. "I have an idea. You look real beat. Maybe you should go back to your apartment first and get refreshed, and then we can do this if you still feel up to it."

"But what about you? It wouldn't be nice to just make you sit around and wait for me..."

Darcy nodded towards her actual personal car. “I always carry a change of clothes with me. I can just follow you to your place and change with you. Sound like a deal?”

“Deal.”

She had no intentions of jumping the rookie. She had no intentions of doing anything but taking her out and buying her a drink to talk about her day until she felt better.

That just wasn’t what happened.

“Nice place you have here,” Darcy commented as kindly as she could about the shabby little apartment complex, and followed Serena up the walk and inside to her door.

The moment they were both inside, her body took over. Shutting the door, she dropped her gym bag of spare clothes, grabbed Serena’s wrists with both hands, and pressed their lips together hard.

The contact was hot and sweet, subtle and passionate. Serena's lips were so soft and just slightly dry, quivering beneath hers.

Darcy's head spun with delight, a hazy rush of sexuality nearly knocking her off her feet. It was all she could do to pull back, to break apart the kiss instead of sliding her tongue in to make it all deeper, and even then she was practically shuddering with effort. Serena's doe-brown eyes were wide as hell, making her look so fucking sweet and innocent that her pussy started throbbing so hard she couldn't ignore it. Shaking now, her voice quavered like never before as she spoke. "Sorry," was all she could manage.

"Do it again," Serena whispered breathlessly, and Darcy did.

Those soft lips parted beneath hers, allowing her tongue entrance. A moan left her throat with pure delight, and she explored the other's mouth with reckless abandon, enjoying the warm, wet sweetness as she discovered all there was to be found. Serena's hands clutched first at her shoulders but then began to slide their way down her back, caressing her muscles and curves before cupping her ass cheeks in small palms.

"Oh," Serena said, sounding a little surprised. "That's nice. Soft."

Darcy laughed. She felt so high on lust it was practically love already. "I'm going to guess you've never been with a woman, huh?"

"Been thinking about it."

"Well, babe," Darcy said, sliding her lips from Serena's mouth to her ear, "this is the time to stop thinking and start *doing*."

With reverent hands, they undressed each other through a rain of kisses and fervent touching, as if they couldn't get enough of each other. And Darcy delighted in every bit of it, maybe even more than Serena did as she made new discoveries in her journey of lesbianism. All over again, she was experiencing how it felt to be tender and unrushed towards release. She wanted to make this special. She wanted to make it last. She could hardly bear the suspense of it all as she slowly undid Serena's hair and then combed it down from the back of her head in luxurious waves, teasing her nipples with the silky tips until she whimpered. Yet, at the same time, she just couldn't get it enough.

Silently, she begged for it to never end as she took in the other woman's naked body for the first time. Petite and pert, she was gorgeous from the ruffled top of her head to the toes on her tiny feet.

I am definitely in way over my head, she thought, and then reached out to take the other's hand in hers. Even that felt impossibly good, as their fingers twined together in a manner somehow much more intimate than sex ever would be. "Bedroom?" she asked, breathless. She hoped the answer was yes, before her pussy juices started dripping down her thighs.

"Okay," Serena said, her teeth practically chattering she was shaking so hard from excitement. Even though it was her apartment, she made no move to lead so Darcy tightened her hold on her hand and guided her in the direction of the only hallway. It was a short hall, leading to a bathroom and a laundry area, and what could only be a bedroom.

The bedroom was tiny and simple, perfectly petite just like its owner. The bed was done up in girly, floral sheets and littered with a smattering of stuffed animals. The rest of the room was more bare and ordinary, surprisingly sparse with only a handful of perfume bottles and makeup supplies lying around. Not a bit of lotion in sight.

Good thing we won't be doing anything that requires lube tonight, Darcy thought, and gently pushed Serena down onto her back in bed.

"Wait," the young woman protested, trying to sit back up. "I want to..."

Darcy lightly touched a finger to her lips. "Let me take care of it. Okay? I want to make you feel good." She kissed Serena sweetly and then started to slowly work her way down the other woman's body, pressing wet little open-mouthed kisses everywhere she could reach.

"But I want to make you feel good, too."

That touched her far more than it should have, so she straightened up and lightly touched her soaking wet pussy. Serena lifted up her head to watch, and then let out a soft little gasp as her eyes went round again. “Oh...oh my.”

“You like that, babe?” Darcy murmured, sliding her finger deep within her throbbing folds. Her pussy lips were swollen and trembling, flushed dark red with desire.

“It looks like a flower...” Serena lifted her head higher and spread her own legs to look down between them. “Does mine look like that?”

“Hmm...let me take a closer look.”

Darcy slid back down and reached out to hold onto Serena’s thighs, letting her nails dig into her skin just the slightest bit so she could feel the pressure. A delighted little whimper pulled from between her lips, and then she cried out as Darcy breathed hard on her most secretive place. Her feminine flower began to bloom and swell, becoming dewy with moisture. Sliding a finger into the younger woman’s depths, Darcy wiggled it around and swirled her touch to hit all her inner walls. At first, Serena's pussy muscles were tight but as Darcy stimulated her, they began to relax and allow her to slip another finger deep inside.

"Fuck...Darcy..."

The rookie cop wrapped her fingers in Darcy's short hair and pulled demandingly. "Please...I need..."

I know exactly what you need, sweetie. And fuck, do I want to give it to you.

Darcy slowly wiggled her finger back out of Serena's pussy. Holding her tight again, with her hands cupping her ass now, she began first by just lightly licking the juices beading up and dripping down the folds of her pussy. She tasted absolutely divine, like the sweetest nectar oozing from the world's rarest flower.

She had missed this, this act of savoring. She couldn't help it, licking slowly deeper and longer to coax more of Serena's juices into her mouth. Her eyes were closed, making sloppy-wet sucking sounds as she delved deeper into her pussy. Deeper and deeper, until her tongue was sliding through the folds and into the depths beyond.

Her upper lip hit Serena's clit. A little cry left her lips, followed by a sharper scream when pleasure took over.

It was like Darcy lost her mind at that! She started fucking her tongue inside Serena's pussy real deep, swirling it around to hit every part of her, straining to reach back as far as she could. Her own pussy was getting closer and closer to exploding without even being touched.

And then, just like that, Serena's muscles clamped down around her tongue as she started to cum heavily, violently. A powerful scream tore from her lips, and then she clawed her fingers through her hair, down her neck and back.

"Fuck!" she screamed.

Still holding onto her with one hand, Darcy shoved a finger inside herself and started to cum as well. The waves of her orgasm rocked through her, shaking her to her very core until she lost herself entirely.

When she finally came back to herself, she was curled up in the middle of the bed with Serena tangled up in her arms, looking shell-shocked. Her breath was slow and deep, her eyes half-shut. Her lips were slightly swollen from being kissed so hard.

Darcy reached up and gently caressed her cheek. A new warmth began to form in her chest, snuggling tentatively into the dark cavern there which she had thought would never be filled again.

"So," she whispered.

Serena turned her head towards her slightly, and blinked a little to signal that she was paying attention.

Darcy kept softly stroking her face, taking a gentler sort of pleasure from the touch. "Why don't you tell me all about what happened today? Don't leave anything out."

Chapter Seven

The next morning was an unusual one for Serena. Even before opening her eyes, before she quite remembered what happened, she knew something was different. Her bed was much the same, warm sheets pulled up almost all the way over her head, and a stuffed animal tucked securely in her arms. All that was right. All that was good and correct, but even so there was something different.

What is it, she asked herself, and opened her eyes. Nothing unusual in front of her, just her shadow cast on the wall from the sunlight streaming in through the blinds behind her. And then she heard it: soft, measured breathing. And then she felt it, the comforting press of a body cuddled against hers from behind. That was what seemed so strange to her. Not once before this had she ever actually shared a bed with anyone. Had sex in one, but never slept together afterwards. It felt good and sweet, like cuddling a puppy.

A fraction of an inch at a time, she slowly moved closer to the other edge of the bed and then rolled over so she could take in the sight. Sweet emerald eyes closed and fluttering just the slightest bit from the snare of dreams, Darcy had her face pressed half against the pillow with her lips ever so slightly parted.

The memory of what that soft mouth could do to her made her pussy start burning with desire. She ignored it partly because she was never one for morning sex, but also because she wanted to just look at the woman in her bed a little longer.

The normally perfect hair was mussed wildly, standing up like a rooster's crest. Her shoulders were bare, as both of them were completely naked beneath the covers. The shape of her body was outlined under them, so tempting that she had to reach out and stroke her fingers over them ever so slightly to keep from waking her. Her fingertips tingled and she couldn't help what came next, a caress of the shoulder, and then a gentle hold on her chin. Something was coming over her, and she lightly touched her lips to Darcy's.

This was probably one of the best sleeps the veteran cop had had in the past week or so, Serena realized, and gently released her chin. It was still early, so best to let her rest for as long as possible. Relaxing back down into the mattress again, she closed her eyes even though she knew sleep wouldn't come. The longer she was awake, the more her thoughts began to circle.

As good as this felt, the reality was that she had no idea about her sexuality still. Her bi-curiousness didn't seem to have faded any, but that didn't mean she was actively bisexual or a lesbian, did it? And it seemed like there was more going on here, because she'd had plenty of sex before this –but not as good, for sure!- that didn't end up so sweetly as this. This was something else entirely. This had the makings of a relationship written all over it. A *good* relationship, too. She could feel it. Darcy was the kind of woman who would give her all and everything to a relationship, who would ride it out to the very end. And Serena could tell from the tugging in her heart that she so badly wanted to do the same. She wanted this to work out. She wanted this to be the sort of organic fairytale love that grew from work, to friendship, to growing old together and being buried beside each other in cemetery plots, but good sex didn't mean a good life.

Enjoying friction and the act of fucking didn't mean she was going to be capable of living a lesbian relationship. Add to that the fact that she knew most cop relationships –whether it was two cops, or a cop and a regular person- ended in separation...she couldn't do that to Darcy. Hell, she couldn't do that to anyone but with Darcy it made her mind scream with wrongness. She was too precious for that, all while denying she was precious right up until the day she died, probably.

Which meant Serena had to nip this in the bud before it was too late.

But not yet. Let me just enjoy this for a little while longer.

So she lay there for another hour, dozing in and out of a peaceful sleep. When her eyes were open, she was taking in the magic of a sleeping woman. And when they were closed, she dreamed of what was never going to be.

Her alarm went off at 7 a.m. She'd been awake for it, so she reached out and quickly shut it off again. Beside her, Darcy was stirring and then sitting up so that the covers fell down her body, exposing her breasts.

At some point last night, Serena had fondled those. They were softer than her own and a size bigger, more than just a handful. And her nipples were velvet soft...

"Good morning," Serena said awkwardly.

Darcy looked at her and smiled a little. "Is it a good morning? Be honest with me, babe."

I can't tell her yet. Look at her.

Serena looked down at her hands, hoping the look was demure rather than ashamed. "I've...I've never had anything like that before. Maybe next time I can do you?"

Why did I say that? Now she'll be expecting more.

Truthfully, more would be more than fine with her but she couldn't do that, dammit.

"We'll see," Darcy said fondly, and patted her cheek before softly kissing her on the lips. She relished in the contact, savoring it. Who knew if it would be the last time they ever did that? "But, I am glad you liked it. It's been a long time since I've had it that good."

"But I didn't even touch you. I wish you'd let me touch you." She cut off the rest of the thought, the rest of the wish that said she would remember it for years, long after they were parted.

"No, but you were really responsive. Some girls just lie there like a dead fish, I swear." Darcy shook her head. "What time is it? 7? Want to shower and I'll make some breakfast?"

"But when will you shower?"

The appraising look Darcy gave her made her realize exactly what the request meant. “Oh! Okay.”

She thought that might mean more sex, but she was to be surprised about that. It was better than sex. Hell, it was almost better than cuddling up to her in bed. It was warm and soapy-slick, with the water pounding down warmly on their tired muscles like the most refreshing rain in the world.

Darcy handed Serena the bar of soap sitting on the inner lip of the tub. “Want to get me all nice and clean?”

“I...I don’t think that’s possible for...for such a dirty girl like you,” Serena said lamely, and then winced. Sexy talk wasn’t her thing. Luckily, the other cop found it amusing.

“Please never say that again.”

Serena nodded. “Trust me, I won’t.” Taking the bar of soap in hand, she started to slide it gently all over Darcy’s body, enjoying the lay of her curves and how the other woman arched against her hand, clearly enjoying herself. When there were suds running all over her body, streaming down over her breasts and to between her legs, she set the soap down on the edge of the tub again and used her hands. She lavished attention on her nipples, rubbed luxuriously up between her legs until the other woman was moaning and grabbing at her wrists.

“Oh, babe...Don’t do that. I’ll have to jump you and then we’ll both be late for work.”

“I wonder if anyone on patrol saw your car parked outside?” Serena wondered suddenly aloud, as she traded places with Darcy to start rinsing her off and get her own soaping-up.

“Hmm...I wouldn’t think so.” Darcy shook her head. “In any case, it’s not like they sat and watched and know it was there all night. A patrol is a patrol, and not a watch on the same narrow area. If you get me.”

“I think I do,” Serena said, nodding emphatically. She wasn’t prepared for what the other woman did next, wrapping her arms around her to slide the bar of soap down deep between her ass cheeks. “Oh...”

“Don’t worry,” she murmured, and withdrew the soap after a moment. “Just getting you clean all over, babe.”

Trust me, I wasn’t worried at all.

After a little bit longer in the shower, they stepped out and dried each other off. Serena thoroughly enjoyed watching Darcy style her hair with a few controlled flicks of her fingers and a well-placed spritz of hair spray; then she stood there and leaned her hip against the counter while watching her finish drying and styling her much-longer hair.

“I have no idea how you have the patience for that,” Darcy commented. “My hair freezes in the winter.”

“That’s bad for your hair.”

“I’ll shave it off and start over,” Darcy replied, and then reached out to caress a handful of Serena’s long brown hair. “But then that means there won’t be anything for you to hold onto.”

Serena closed her eyes under the pretense of pain as she wrapped her hair up into a bun, hiding her grimace. Why was she going to make this so hard to do?

After finishing getting ready, they headed out to the kitchen where Darcy proceeded to somehow make them both breakfast despite the fact that Serena really didn't have much of anything at all. She never did. Necessities were necessities and that was all she ever bought. When she ran out, she would buy more. Every other meal was either obtained while out on patrol, going to work, or coming back from it.

Yet somehow, Darcy managed to magically procure half a loaf of bread to go along with their eggs and milk, discovered a skillet deep in the back of one cupboard, and somehow also managed to find cinnamon.

Serena shook her head. "I honestly have no idea how that got here."

"It's almost like magic," Darcy commented, dipping a slice of bread into the mixture and then dropping it into the skillet, where it began to hiss and fry up. “Lots of people don’t remember ever buying any spices but they have them anyway. It’s almost like it’s a never-ending chain of people leaving theirs behind and someone else getting them when they move in.”

The rest of their conversation was equally light and insignificant as Darcy continued to make French toast. Serena busied herself too, making a pot of coffee. In the end, the coffee sucked and the toast was somehow fantastic even with only about a tablespoon of syrup left in the container to share between them.

“This has been really nice,” Serena said, feeling more awkward than she probably should have. The moment was approaching and with each passing second, she felt more and more like this was going to be a terrible decision. But what else could she do?

“But?”

“But what? What makes you think there’s a but?”

"There's always a but." Darcy looked down, sighing into her mug. "So, you might as well get it over with and tell me what it is. What have I done wrong this time? I didn't even push it too quickly. We've known each other for months."

"I know." Her heart started aching. "It's not that. And I swear it's not you. I swear. I know people always say that but this time it really isn't you. It really is me. I just don't know about myself."

"Ever had sex that good before?" Darcy said darkly. "Because I have had a lot of sex and none of it was quite that good."

"I've had a lot of sex, too!" Serena said, and then blushed a little bit. That definitely wasn't something she felt she should be shouting to the rooftops when her neighbors' rooms weren't that far away. "And you're right. It was fucking awesome. But that doesn't mean anything."

"What, you always have sex with people who don't mean anything?"

“Darcy!” Tears sprang to her eyes. “Stop it and just let me explain, okay? I like you a lot. I think I like you a lot more than I’ve liked a lot of other people. Maybe even more than anyone else, ever. I liked having sex with you. I like spending time with you. I think you’re beautiful. But I don’t know if I’m gay, okay? I don’t know if I’m a lesbian. I think...I’ve been feeling bi-curious for a while but I don’t know if I actually am. And I don’t know if I’d be able to have a lesbian relationship with you or anyone else. Please tell me you understand that.”

Darcy seemed to regard her mug for a while longer before eventually looking up. “It kind of seems to me like the only way to find out would be to have one.”

“But if we have one and then it gets all fucked up because I figure out that I’m not really ready or that I just can’t? Don’t you see that it would hurt way more at that point than if we break this off right now?”

“I don’t know,” Darcy said. “What’s worse? Having something and then losing it, or never knowing if you would have ever had something?” And then she sighed. “But, I understand. For you, I understand. We’ll just be friends, okay?”

"Are you sure?"

"Is that what you want?"

Serena just shook her head in response.

"Then, that's what we have to do. I understand it, so we have to do it or else you won't ever be happy as long as you're still questioning. But you have to promise me that if you think you've ever got it figured out...well, tell me. Please, okay?"

"I will," Serena said, relieved. "Thank you so much for being so understanding."

"Sure."

They finished the rest of their breakfast in silence, and then they headed out to the station to go on patrol. They arrived separately, a few minutes off from each other so that no one could suspect them of anything.

There were no goodbyes. There were no handshakes or hugs or wishing-wells. All of that was implied and unnecessary, because they were still going to be friends. Just...not lovers.

As she pulled away from the station in her cruiser to head out on the route she had come to know as "hers," Serena was once again hit with that feeling that things were wrong. But at this point, what else could she do?

She wasn't very long into the patrol when an alert came over the radio. "I need all available officers to head over to 175 Oakvale Parkway," the dispatcher said calmly.

A quick glance at her GPS confirmed for her that she was very close by. A little sigh left her lips. *Fantastic.* Why did it seem like she had all the bad luck with arriving to places first?

Considering how many officers there were on the force though, she suspected she really didn't have it all that bad. It would have just been nice to have the rest of this awful day to spend not really thinking about or doing anything. Oh well. At least all this activity meant she would have some calm days coming up soon.

Picking up the mouthpiece as she picked up her speed, she said, "Cruiser 119, Officer Blake. I am only a few blocks away and will be there in a moment. What's going on?"

"Officer Blake!" the dispatcher said, their voice rising with the first true bit of emotion that she'd ever heard from them. The difference wasn't quite enough for her to get a grasp on whether it was a man or a woman, though. "Congrats on that drunk driving catch. Real well done. Anyway," they continued, snapping back into professionalism, "We got a 911 call. A woman on the line who said she's scared her husband is going to kill her. She said she was in the bedroom and has locked herself inside. Connection was lost, but right before that we heard banging. Emergency services is continuing to call but getting no response."

"Got it," Serena confirmed. Just like that, all thoughts of Darcy were shoved from her mind as she realized the importance of responding to this situation with her mind fully focused on the subject at hand.

A new voice came over the radio. Lieutenant Jacobs, the vibration of her words nearly lost beneath static and the sound of rushing wind as she picked up the speed in her own police car. “Serena, remember protocol. Assess the situation. Observe before acting. I’ll be there as soon as I can. If you can, wait for backup.”

But if I can’t, observe and then act.

“Got it, Lieutenant.”

The last thing she heard before dropping the mouthpiece was a muffled, “Good luck.”

I’m going to need it, she thought, and made the quick decision not to turn on her lights or her siren. If there was a confrontation going on, a life or death situation, she needed the element of stealth on her side.

175 Oakvale turned out to be in a cute little neighborhood that was a little more high-end than the places she’d been prowling

around for the past months. All the houses were actual houses, with moderately well-maintained yards and decorations that the owners could obviously rely on to not be stolen from out beneath their noses. She spotted some newer model cars, too.

The actual house itself was one of the rare two-story houses in the neighborhood, with a newer model car and a fence around a backyard which seemed to contain an entire forest. These folks were pretty upscale.

Parking as quietly as she could, blocking off the driveway with her cruiser, Serena stepped out of the car with her pistol already drawn and the safety off. Keeping it pointed towards the ground just in case anything happened to surprise her, she crouched down slightly and approached the front door. So far, nothing seemed out of the ordinary. No yelling and screaming, no sounds of a struggle from within.

Of course, that could be either good or bad depending on the actual situation.

Luckily there was no window between her and the front door, but it was also unlucky in that she couldn't even try to glimpse through to get a read on the interior.

The front door was unlocked, because of course it was.

Serena lifted up her gun just the slightest so a bullet fired off would nail the legs of anyone who rushed her.

The foyer right in front of her was delightfully clean, without a single bit of mud in sight. All the shoes on the rack were in a nice, neat little array. Directly ahead of her was a living room, while a hallway went off to the right side and a staircase rose up on her left.

A quick look around determined that there was no sign of a struggle down here. At the same moment as she was looking around, a resounding thump came from upstairs.

"Shit," she swore, and lifted up her pistol all the way just in time for someone to come tumbling recklessly down the steps. Her trigger finger twitched, jumping so hard that she very nearly pulled on it before managing to stop herself. It was a woman, her hair all disheveled and her clothes an utter mess.

She looked up when she was halfway down the stairs, grabbing at the railing to stop herself from falling. And then her eyes went wide and she let go of the rail to put her hands up in the air defensively. “Stop, don’t shoot!” she pleaded, voice cracking.

Serena flipped her safety back on for just a moment, jamming her gun down into the holster again to reach out one hand to the terrified woman. “I am a police officer,” she said, trying to sound commanding and caring while ignoring the fact she was being obvious. Of course she was a police officer. Duh. “My name is Serena Blake. Please come with me, ma’am.”

The scared woman grabbed onto her hand and allowed herself to be hurried on down from the stairs. “My name...I...I’m Maggie.”

Serena guided her out of the house, watching their back with her pistol out again. No one was following them.

"Maggie, would you like to tell me what's going on? I'm just going to give you a seat here in my cruiser, okay? Is that fine?"

Maggie nodded and took a deep breath through racing tears. "I...he's been...he's been real abusive towards me lately and...and he got out his gun..."

"Did he have his gun when you ran down the stairs?" she tried to make her voice urgent, to somehow get the message across that they needed to hurry in this situation.

"I...I pushed him. He fell and I ran."

That didn't tell her much. It told her that the husband probably still had the safety flipped on, otherwise she probably would have heard the shot when he fell. And it also said that he was going to be pissed.

"Okay, ma'am. I'm going to go in and take care of your husband. You stay here, okay?"

She didn't give Maggie a chance to say anything else, and quickly shut the door. Cop cars were incapable of being opened from the inside, so she wouldn't be able to endanger herself this way. She wished that she would be able to keep the woman with her while having a standoff with the husband, so that she would know she was safe, but that was completely impossible.

Grabbing at the passenger side door now, she ignored Maggie's frantic questions and pulled the mouthpiece to her lips. "Lieutenant Jacobs," she said, "I have the wife safe and in my cruiser. The husband is still inside. I'm going after him. I'll be safe."

Turning off the radio, she looked to the backseat at Maggie. "What's your husband's name?"

"Thomas!"

"Okay, thank you. My back-up will be here soon, okay? They'll take care of you. I'm going in after your husband."

Once again closing the door before any protests could reach her ears, Serena gripped her gun hard and headed back across the lawn and up to the house again.

Chapter Eight

"Lieutenant Jacobs," she said, "I have the wife safe and in my cruiser. The husband is still inside. I'm going after him. I'll be safe."

Her heart froze when she heard Serena's soft, serious voice say those words. Every part of her being cried out against it, to the point where she almost screamed it out loud. The rookie managed to pull off something absolutely incredibly just yesterday but that didn't mean she was going to be able to keep the same insane sort of luck that let her pull all those risky maneuvers when she was chasing the drunk driver.

After having sex was when they discussed the events of her day. The whole way through the story of that drunk driver, even though she knew the outcome was plain miraculous, Darcy had to hold back her winces and exclamations of concern, especially when the rookie was so overcome with memories of all the risks she'd taken that she actually started to weep purely from being overwhelmed by the sheer scale of it all. And she was right to weep, Darcy thought. It *was* miraculous. Those moves she pulled were deadly. Completely in the book, and 100% legal, which meant there was no way any flack was ever going to come back against her about it, but every step of the way, someone could have died. The driver could have died. Serena could have died. Any number of those dozens of cars they passed could have been the ones to die. That was just how the life of a cop panned out sometimes. But the fact that nothing had happened...

Something was going to happen tonight. Darcy was absolutely certain of it. And they were still friends. Friends and former partners. She really didn't want anything to happen to one of the best people to ever come into her life, and especially not someone like Serena. The woman was strong but she didn't want there to be any chance that something like this would dampen her fervor for life, her pleasure for existing. That happened to the ones who stuck around for awhile, and Darcy would rather the realization come about organically instead of in such a short period. That would crush her for a *lot* of things, not just policing.

Breaking through the numbness which had seized her whole being, Darcy pulled over to the side of the road and tried to assess the circumstances. Because patrol routes were constantly swapped around, she knew the whole of Hartford like the back of her hand. The location was halfway across the city for her. There was no way she was going to make it in time to be able to help for anything.

It's not the skilled people who are deadliest, it's the uneducated idiots. That husband could really fuck things up if he wanted to. A gun was a tool of death in anyone's hands.

Very dimly, she heard a reply from Jacobs come over the radio. "Don't make any stupid moves," she said. The harshness in her voice stood out even through the static. Drunk driving could result in a pass even if the officer who screwed things up was found to be at fault, because no one liked drunk drivers. But in domestic disputes? The media was all over those. The news was always on the side of the victim, which meant if they messed anything up for the victim they would be in super-hot water.

No response from Serena, which meant she was already gone.

Fuck, Darcy thought and pulled back out into the street again. She knew if she drove like a maniac now, her judgment was going to be impaired by her worry. The Lieutenant and other members of backup would arrive shortly. They would arrive and make sure nothing bad happened until she could get there –she just had to make sure that she would be alive to get there.

Her shoulders tensed up and her whole body was a tangle of nerves as she continued to drive at an agonizingly-slow pace to the location. Even speeding by over ten mph, earning herself honks from drivers who only realized at the last second that she was a cop, she felt like she was going too slow.

Her windows were done and she strained her hearing while driving. However, even if she had them down she would have still been able to hear the sound of a gun being fired off. “Shit,” she swore, and slammed her palm against the steering wheel. “Shit, shit!”

A nerve-grinding two minutes later, Darcy pulled up out front of the two-story house. Well, not quite in front. She found that she had to park nearly half a block away due to the sheer number of other cops who had arrived and the media vans. Many of the officers currently in the area were fielding reporters, forming blockades. It was with a sinking feeling that Darcy realized she was going to have to join them. She was a beat cop, not a Serena-protector. Her duty should be to everyone equally, not to only one person like this that had been the whole reason she showed up.

Getting out of her cruiser, she was immediately accosted by a red-haired reporter wearing way too much blush. A cameraman followed her around, nearly stepping on her heels every foot of the way.

“Excuse me! Excuse me, officer!” the reporter said, and stuck her microphone in Darcy’s face. “Can you give us a statement on the incident, please?”

Darcy glowered at her. “What, you think I have something to say when I literally just got here? Please.”

She turned her back and started heading over to the nearest cop, to see if she could find the Lieutenant. From behind her she heard a disdainful murmur of, “Ugly bitch dyke,” and ignored it. It wouldn’t be the first or last time she’d heard such a thing. Names slid off her back like water now.

The Lieutenant turned out to be standing with the woman who called 911, the wife named Maggie, taking statements as she told the story. At least, that was what she had been doing before the shot went off. Now she was standing silent with the wife crying hysterically beside her, both of them completely focused on the house.

“Is there anyone else inside there with her?” Darcy called out, rushing towards Jacobs.

The gorgeous black woman shook her head. “We got here literally only a few seconds before you. As far as I know, there’s no one else in there. I’ve been trying to get everything under control with the crowds and see what's happened before we got here. Not much luck with that, though." She threw a frustrated glare at the crying wife, who looked too hysterical to provide any actual information. "I was just about to give it up and go in myself but now you're here. Go. Secure the scene. I'll have someone following you in only a few seconds."

While this normally wasn't part of her duties in a situation like this, Darcy relished the chance. She wasn't about to turn it down. "I'm already there."

Drawing her piece as she turned away, she held it in a classic grip and approached the house. No sign of a conflict in the living room, but there was a lamp knocked off a small corner table on the miniature halfway landing between the ground floor and the second floor. Holding up her pistol in front of her, she headed up the stairs. There was no sound, absolutely no sign of anything at all.

There was a bathroom directly in front of the stairwell when she reached the second floor. The light was off in there, though the hallway lights were on. In fact, all the room lights – the extras were guestroom and storage, she assumed- were off but for one. The master bedroom presumably.

“This is Officer Darcy Fairweather,” she called softly. “I’m coming in.”

No answer.

She headed forward and through the entryway.

The first thing she saw was blood. Blood sprayed up one wall, and the wide feet of a man sticking out from the opposite side of the bed on the floor below, where she couldn’t see the rest of him.

And the second thing she noticed was that Serena stood to the side of her, gun drawn. She could feel the heat emanating from the muzzle. Her face was blank, the perfect picture of shock and brokenness.

Scene secured, Darcy thought.

Chapter Nine

I killed him. I shot that man.

Those were the only words in her mind, a mantra which stayed with her all through the process afterwards. It was a straightforward process but Serena felt like every single moment, the detectives who arrived to assess the scene were judging her and casting blame. She tried to console herself, to insist to herself that things like this happened all the time, that this was the reason police officers existed, but it hardly helped.

She would never forget the stunned look Darcy gave her when she looked at her after noticing the corpse. It was a pained expression of realization, what this might mean for her. The most horrid of thoughts burst through her mind: prison, losing her job, failing her brother...

A shiver had run through her when she looked at Darcy but it didn't pass. It didn't simply run its course and then leave her with only a ghostly memory. It continue to rattle around inside her whole body, continuing to shake her. Her teeth were chattering. Her hands were shaking around the gun and she went to lift it, to turn off the safety before anything bad happened.

As simple as anything, the older cop plucked the pistol out of her hands and flipped the safety off, and then tucked it into her holster. "You'll hurt someone waving that around like that," she said. Serena nodded blankly, and then Darcy put her hands on her shoulders; the warmth of her touch was like a beacon on a dark night, slicing through the cold which gripped her. "Answer this question. Yes or no. Was he going to shoot?"

She nodded, not able to find her voice.

"You have to tell me. Say it out loud."

Licking her lips a little, Serena tried again and managed to get her lips to work enough to say, “Y-yes...”

“Where?”

That question seemed to come from a little further away, the warmth of Darcy’s touch fading. She felt her legs wobble, knew she was starting to lose her grip on herself. Whiteness fuzzed at the edge of her vision, slowly pressing inward. And then she was being shaken roughly back and forth, just once or twice very fiercely, but it shook away the cobwebs which had been forming and allowed her to stand on her own feet again. Even if it was just a protest to the fact that she was being shaken, she was standing up straight now.

She echoed dully, “Where?”

“Yeah. Where was he aiming? Where was he going to shoot you, Serena? You’re the sharpshooter. Where?”

“I...I’m not sure.”

“Well,” Darcy lowered her voice, “you better damn sure *be* sure real quick because while I don’t see this causing too big of a stir just because of who that asshole is –and you’re both white, so that’s good- because he’s a nobody but you need to get your story straight. You *need* to know, here and now, what happened. Where was he going to shoot you?”

Serena closed her eyes and focused back on the past few seconds even though she really didn’t want to, just vainly hoping that it would all be over soon. “His gun was up high. My head or my heart. He was close enough to do it too, and he held it like he knew what he was doing.”

“So it was self-defense on your part?”

“Yes,” she confirmed. Though the rest of the details were just too blurry, too *soon* for her to get a good grip on right now, she knew it was self-defense. He would have killed her if she hadn’t killed him.

Still she couldn’t stop replaying that dreadful moment over and over in her mind, the click of the trigger as her finger pulled in all the way and the split second of contact, followed by splatters and then a huge thump. She saw the bullet hole form in the front of his forehead, saw the splash of scarlet explode up behind him.

Over and over, no matter how tightly she shut her eyes to try and block it out. The truth was that this came from inside her and now she had no idea when she would ever be rid of it.

There wasn't much longer to go on simply with thinking and pondering, because just then they heard the sound of footsteps as someone entered the house and began to take the steps two at a time.

"In here," Darcy called, and moved over slightly to peek out the doorway. "Oh, it's you, Lieutenant. You had better get the crime scene crews up here to take care of this because he's been shot down."

Serena heard the Lieutenant curse loudly from down the hall. "Damn rookie."

"Hey!" she protested. That had been like a stab to the heart.

Jacobs appeared in the doorway now and took a moment to glance over at the scene. She stepped a few feet closer than the two other women had been before backing up to rejoin them. "Calm down, Blake," she said, her voice a little softer now. "As long as you tell the truth about all this, we're in the clear. Plus, the world is down one abuser. In jail, he would have done some time and probably gotten out early. I know these rich idiots. But to tell you the truth, I prefer seeing him down like this."

"O...kay," she said reluctantly. At least both of these veterans had told her the same thing. That was good. It meant she didn't have to try to pick or choose which person she was going to listen to, but damn, she wished it hadn't turned out like this.

She followed Darcy out of the room when the Lieutenant told her to go, and they headed back outside to where the media presence had strengthened with the arrival of an ambulance. Apparently Maggie had been beaten on pretty badly before she was able to call the cops, with some bruises showing in the red and blue lights which Serena hadn't noticed before. She was going to head to the hospital with a police escort to make sure she got in safely without being hounded.

“Okay,” Darcy said calmly, as they watched the ambulance head out with a cruiser in front of and behind it. “Now that’s taken care of, we can get started with the rest of this. Lieutenant will be calling some detectives in to go over the crime scene. What they’ll do is ask you how everything went and you tell them in excruciating detail every single thing that you did. Then, they go in and do their work, while we stay out here and play round ‘em up.”

Serena followed Darcy still, sticking right behind her like a lost duckling. “What does that mean? We have to get the media to leave?”

“Not leave, necessarily. Hey! Off the fucking grass!”

“Hey!” a reporter snapped back, frozen halfway across the lawn. Dusk was falling and it was getting harder and harder to see. “Watch your fucking language, okay? Now we can’t use anything we shot right now with you screaming in the background.”

"That was the *plan,* numbnuts," Darcy snarled. "Now get off the grass. You're trespassing on someone's private property."

Grumbling incredibly irritably, the reporter trudged back to the sidewalk and stood there sulking. A camera turned in his direction and he was about to speak when another cop came rushing forward from the opposite direction. "You idiots can't film here. You have the permission of these homeowners to film with their places in the background? And don't go disturbing anyone just to do that!"

Serena sat back and watched with a bit of awe while Darcy pointed out more occasions of this happening all around them. It was like watching children chase seagulls on a beach. Where one was taking off, another was landing; while that one was landing, the first and three more came wheeling back in. There was no end to it.

"This is madness. Holy shit. I had no idea."

"They have to be like this to get anything. They've got a job too, but unfortunately it's one that kind of contradicts ours." Darcy shrugged. "I just wish they weren't all such idiotic animals. But, if you ever need them to back off *real* bad, cuss at them. It'll come back to bite you in the ass on our end –but not too badly, because our superiors get it more than other bosses- but they all air on family-friendly networks. They can't use anything with cussing and it takes too much time to edit the beeps in. So, go on and get out there, Serena. Start doing some crowd control."

But I just want to go home.

Darcy had been turning away, but must have seen the look cross her face anyway. "I'm sorry. You have to stay for now. I know you just want to leave, and I'll cover for you as soon as we get our other units back from their visit to the hospital, but until then..."

She understood. Didn't like it, but she understood.

For the next hour, she experienced the action of chasing birds just like she had when she was a child. It was much, much less fun this time when she was surrounded by the birds, and they could talk, and call her names, and flash lights in her face, and follow her around with cameras while she was going after other birds. It was, however, just as noisy as she remembered it. And frustrating. So very frustrating.

But eventually the other officers did come back. She hardly noticed, because at that point she was just so busy focusing on putting one foot down in front of the other that she hardly cared what anyone was actually doing. Exhaustion dragged at her for the second time in as many times.

All this excitement is seriously going to do me in, I swear. I don't know how I'm going to surprise this.

Someone tapped on her shoulder and she practically leapt three feet into the air, spinning around with her hand clamped on the butt of her pistol.

It was Darcy, distinct only in the play of lights over her hair and the way the shadows caught in her facial structure. "Serena? They're here. I'm reliving you."

"Are you sure?" she asked, rubbing at her eyes. The chance to leave and get some sleepy was right there in front of her but she couldn't leave the situation like this if she needed to be there.

"I'm sure. I've got you covered, don't worry. Just...don't even go back to the station. Just head straight home in the cruiser, okay? And be sure to tell some people that you're going home –straight home- on the way out."

"Thank you."

But the other cop had already turned away. Beyond caring, Serena headed over to where she was parked, making sure to grab two or three other cops on the way out. All of them gave her noncommittal well-wishes to have a good night, telling her that none of them knew she was the one who shot the husband, Thomas. She had spoken to those detectives when they came out to get her while chasing reporters, but apparently they were better at keeping secrets than anyone else she knew, if none of these other cops had a reason to be suspicious of her.

But they *didn't* have a reason to be suspicious, she tried to soothe herself. They really didn't. He'd been aiming to kill her, had been so fucking furious with her presence and the fact that she was a cop that he hadn't even bothered to talk to her. He hadn't said a word. Just lifted his gun with his finger on the trigger.

Like she had done months ago in the shooting range with Darcy, she dropped into position and fired off a shot that took him out. Maybe she should have nailed him in the hand or the shoulder but those wouldn't have guaranteed a stop.

I really hope I did the right thing.

Before long, she reached her apartment and dragged her sorry, worn-out ass up the stairs and into her living room. Every part of her ached to just fall face-first on the floor but she knew that was no way to take care of herself, so she heated up some French toast, brushed her teeth and washed her face, and then, only then, did she allow herself to fall into bed. Just like that, she was out.

Chapter Ten

The next morning, Serena rose to her alarm with a groan. Part of her very badly wanted to just give up on all this and call in sick, but that would be extremely unethical and bad practice even if she *did* feel a little sick. She'd hardly slept at all, wavering in and out of horrible dreams where it was just the memory of shooting Thomas over and over again.

Honestly though, even if she did choose to stay home and lounge around in bed all day, it wouldn't make her feel any better if she just kept being unable to sleep. Maybe it was just better to go to work and have a lot of coffee all day to keep her going, and then collapse into bed at the end of it all. Maybe if she wore herself down enough, she could actually sleep the next night. And then after that it would be her day off...

Grabbing her phone to finally turn off the alarm, she saw that she had a new text. *Who could that be from?* She wondered groggily. She hadn't had anyone text her in a very long time except for...

Of course it was Darcy.

"How are you feeling?" the text read.

Serena got up and started texting as she headed out to the kitchen, her thumbs a wobbly blur on the screen. "I feel like death," she started to type, and then winced. But there wasn't much more of an accurate statement, was there? Mentally shrugging, she finished the text and then made some very strong coffee while heating up the last of the French toast. Darcy had answered by the time everything was ready, so she leaned her hip against the counter and read the reply while sipping coffee.

"Understandable. Just be prepared for anything today throws at you."

Serena frowned. What was that supposed to mean? Did Darcy know something about what happened last that she didn't? Of course, that wasn't impossible, was it? After all, who knew how late the other cop had been there, taking care of things? She decided to ask that and then sent the text.

It wasn't until she was done eating breakfast and drying her hair from her shower –and remembering fondly how Darcy seemed fascinated by the sheer quantity- that her phone's screen lit up again with another reply.

"Too late. Ha. But anyway, just be ready. Talk to you later."

If "too late" was as late as she thought it was, then that meant Darcy should have still been asleep. That also then meant that she had set an alarm specifically to be up right now to talk.

Incredibly touched that the other woman would go through such measures for her even though they had broken off their "relationship," Serena touched her heart. Darcy was just a good person through and through.

"I will, I promise. Get some sleep. I..." She stopped. "Fuck," she said aloud, because she had come very close to typing the dreaded L-word.

Backspacing a few times, she sent the text and then hopped into the cruiser. It felt weird to be driving to work in a vehicle that was only hers in the barest sense of the word, but it ended soon enough as she parked in the lot and saw her old truck waiting faithfully for her to come and bring it home. Patting it affectionately on the hood as she walked by, she stepped into the station and found that she was being waited on by the Lieutenant.

"Lieutenant," she said, nodding at her. She started to walk by but was stopped as Jacobs held out one coffee-brown hand to stop her.

"Blake, I need to see you in my office, please."

"Okay?" she asked, but there was no answer forthcoming, so she just shrugged a little and moved forward to follow behind. It seemed like she was doing a lot of following lately, and she wasn't quite sure how she should feel about that; it was like being demoted to rookie status all over again, really. Either way, she could only have her question answered by doing exactly that, so that was what she did.

Jacobs's office was small and cluttered, as were most workspaces where people in uniform were involved. There were discarded coffee cups scattered all over the place, and a majority of the papers lying around also had coffee rings on them. There was a bookshelf filled with crime novels and primers, and law books, and a half-alive potted plant in the corner beside. The Lieutenant's desk was covered in an array of little picture frames, all of which held pictures of animals, or a person and an animal.

A little smile played around the corners of Serena's mouth as she looked around. It didn't look like a clinical sort of place where people would come to spill their secrets, or to be fired. She was especially happy about that last part. No, this looked like a cozy little corner with just enough homey touches to put her at ease.

She shouldn't have let herself be at ease, though.

She turned around to shut the door behind her, only to find there was another person following her in. It was a tall man with broad shoulders, dressed like a detective.

His badge said Detective Flannery. And now that she was looking up from the badge, she saw that his Irish heritage was definitely apparent. His beard was the color of fire, though he was bald on top.

Flannery stuck out his hand. "Hi. Serena Blake, right? You're that rookie kid everyone's been talking about lately, right? It's nice to meet you. I'm Detective Flannery."

Serena gripped his hand, trying her hardest not to let her fingers shake. "It's nice to meet you too," she said, and she released his hand to watch him shut the door to the office. And then it was just the three of them, cut off from the rest of the world. "What's going on?"

Jacobs gestured to one of the chairs in front of her desk. "Please, have a seat, Serena."

When everyone was sitting, the Lieutenant took out a piece of paperwork and pushed it over towards Serena. She tried to figure out what it was but the words swam across the page in front of her eyes. Instead of letting it be obvious how nervous she was, she stroked the edge of the document while pretending to scan it. "What's this?"

"This would be the paper you need to sign so I can place you on temporary leave. Paid, of course."

"But...why? Is it because of..."

Flannery cut in. "Of course it's because of last night. You're in a good bit of trouble, rookie. Not necessarily *bad* trouble, but there's certainly trouble."

Am I going to be arrested? she wanted to ask, but she knew that would only earn her a suspicion-ridden question about if she *should* be arrested. Instead, she said, "I'm not sure that I understand."

"You gave us a statement last night that said you shot the man –the husband Thomas- at the scene because he pulled his gun on you."

“That’s right.”

“We combed all over the scene. There was no gun to be found. And the wife Maggie says that her husband doesn’t even own a gun.”

“But that’s not true! She told me that he had his gun out.”

“Well, whatever she said to you can’t be confirmed as an official statement,” Lieutenant Jacobs said, shaking her head. “I’m sure that this is all some sort of mix-up. You’re a great police officer and the vet who trained you swears by you. And I don’t see a hint of falsehood in you, but until we get all this straightened out, I’m placing you on that temporary leave.”

It felt like the entire world was falling apart around her. She knew what happened. She saw the gun! She saw all of it but...This couldn’t be happening.

But a look back and forth between the two superiors told her that nothing she could say to defend herself would affect this outcome. She just had to accept it.

"Okay," she whispered. Jacobs handed her a pen, and she signed on the line at the bottom. Her hand was shaking so badly that it was barely legible or identifiable as hers, but two witnesses would hold her to it if she tried to deny it being hers. She didn't plan on doing that. She was in more than enough trouble.

Flannery stood and nodded his bald head at her. "Thank you very much for your cooperation, Serena. I'm sure we'll get this all straightened out soon. But just in case, are you always available at that number listed in your application?"

"Yes, sir."

"I might be getting in touch with some questions," he said briskly. "So, if you get a call from an unknown number..."

All she could do was nod, and then he disappeared out the door.

All she could do was stand there, numb and dumbfounded. She barely started her career and now all this...

A surprising amount of warmth suddenly came over her as Lieutenant Jacobs suddenly approached and gave her a very unprofessional and undetached sort of hug. “Don’t worry about this, honey. You’re good people. This will all be sorted out in no time. But for now, take your paperwork with you and fill it out with *exactly* the same details as you’ve said out loud. And then go home and get some rest.”

“Okay,” she said. It took too much effort to remember her manners and say thank you, but somehow she managed.

The walk of shame she took back out of the station was witnessed by exactly one person, and she was certain that was at least ten too many.

The moment she was home, she set the paperwork down on the kitchen counter, curled up in her bed, and picked up her phone to call Darcy.

Chapter Eleven

Darcy knew what the call was about when Serena's number lit up on her phone. Last night after Serena had gone home, Jacobs pulled her aside and asked her what she thought of the rookie.

Darcy looked her right in the eyes. She tried to hide that she had feelings for the other woman but it was difficult, especially when she really did. Lieutenant Jacobs saw it anyway but didn't comment until she was finished speaking. "She's a damn good cop for being so new. A bit...rough around the edges. But by that I mean she thinks she's going to be able to save everyone and make a difference."

"One of those, huh? Well, what do you think? I need your unbiased opinion here, Fairweather."

"My unbiased opinion is that we are not in a relationship, and that she acted with every right to do what she did."

"Good enough for me," the Lieutenant said. "And hopefully we'll get this all sorted out, but we've been wrong before, haven't we? The bad ones think they're doing just as much good."

That was true enough but Darcy knew deep in her heart that the woman she'd had sex with was nothing but good. All this meant she wasn't going to get enough sleep for a bit longer, but she had to do it.

She loved Serena, even if the other woman couldn't love her back. And besides, they were friends. Friends helped friends in times of need even if they didn't have a vested interest in the outcome. That was something the rookie understood as well apparently, because she received the call asking her to come over right about when she thought she would.

"Darcy?" came her fragile voice, blurring with tears.

"Hi, Serena," she said, trying not to sound as if her heart was breaking for the cop. "What's up?"

She hoped the other woman wouldn't be able to tell that she was wide awake, and she was in luck. "I...I really don't want to bother you and I'm sorry that I woke you up but I really need to talk to someone and you're the only person I have. Please."

So, she did what she was planning to do all along and headed over to Serena's apartment, where she listened to the young woman tell a story of a plight she already knew about. She was obviously shaken and terrified, upset about what she'd done and the consequences now, to the point where she was questioning her own judgment.

It was at that point that she stopped her. “You *can’t* doubt yourself, Serena. If you doubt yourself, everyone else will doubt you, too. *That* is what ruins careers, not scandals like this. you have to be able to defend yourself!”

“But it’s so hard because I know how much I’ve fucked up,” the rookie said, wiping her eyes. “Except I know I didn’t but everyone is treating me like it.”

“Yeah? And how many people do you think have gotten strikes against them because the customer lies? But being a police officer is different. We’re doing an actual investigation here, so just stick to the story you told –the *right*- story and everything will be fine in the end.”

She hung around a little longer, until the tears stopped and Serena was consoled enough to be convinced to get some extra sleep –if she was going to get paid for it, why not use all this time to get some sleep?- and then she left. But she didn’t head back to her own place to get some sleep too. No, she had a mission now.

The clean-up crew should have finished in the house, which meant the wife Maggie should have returned home.

Darcy showed up at the scene, which was being watched by only a single police officer in a cruiser parked alongside the street. There weren't even any news vans in sight.

Odd, she thought, and pulled up beside the cruiser. She knew the officer inside pretty well, which was lucky. He rolled down the window for her. "Hey, Darcy! You're off today, right? What brings you to this neighborhood?" He rolled his eyes.

She rolled her eyes right back. "Just can't stay away." The other officer laughed. "Why is it so abandoned here?"

"Well, you know how it is. The lady moved on out, so the hounds chased after her. And then we have to chase after the hounds, so I'm just here holding down the home base."

The wife was driving around the day after her husband was shot and killed? Well, he had been abusive, but in her experience the abused ones were some of the saddest out there when things like this happened to separate them. Bitter, but a reality nonetheless.

“Well, I’m sure you’ll find something to do with your time,” she said.

“Yeah, might just rub one out,” he muttered. “See you later, Darcy.”

“See you,” she said with a smile, which she dropped immediately the moment she was out of sight. Everything about this was starting to get strange. She wished she could have asked what direction the lady had gone in but that would be prying too much, and she didn't want anyone to know she was investigating on her own. Oh well. There was nothing to do for it but to start her search.

Where would a lady who was liberated anew from her deadbeat husband have gone, especially so early in the morning? It was a mystery, but something told her to hit up the shopping district. People who were the inferior in a controlling relationship often had their diet and spending habits constricted. It was just as likely as not that Maggie was out getting herself a fast food breakfast, or shopping for a dress she wasn't allowed to wear before, or simply doing something just to get away.

Although, if she feels liberated, she might not have pressed charges against Serena. Then again, nothing is black and white. She could definitely feel liberated while wanting some extra cash to go along with it.

So, she drove around a few miles under the speed limit, and let herself be amused by the difference in the way other drivers acted around her when she wasn't in her cruiser. They passed by her, with an occasional honk, and she kept her eyes open for anything unusual that might give her a hint as to Maggie's whereabouts.

Fifteen minutes after she began her search, she saw it. Not Maggie's car, which she wouldn't have been able to identify anyway, but a gathering of media vans and police cars in the parking lot of a diner.

Maybe her whole breakfast idea had been right after all.

Navigating through the traffic, she pulled up into the parking lot along the side so that she was out of sight of the other officers, and she sat and waited while looking around.

Maggie stood in front of the diner, arms crossed in front of herself. She didn't look like a victim, even if it was pretty obvious that she was wearing so much makeup just to hide bruises. She looked bored and impatient.

Finally, a new car pulled into the lot and her behavior changed to one of anticipation. A man got out of the car after it was parked. Tall and broad-shouldered, he wore a suit and looked very much like a businessman stopping to get some breakfast on his way to work.

Maggie ran to him as soon as he was in sight, and they embraced deeply. Darcy strained her eyes and ears, and thought she heard Maggie ask, "What took you so long?" but she didn't hear the response.

Either way, this was intriguing. A love interest? A secret boyfriend?

Getting out of the car at the same time as a large group of people were passing her by, Darcy headed inside and quickly scanned the crowd. Maggie and her unidentified friend were both sitting in a section to the left, so she requested the same section.

Now that she was closer –not close enough to hear their conversation through the general din of the restaurant, but certainly close enough to see how they interacted with each other- she observed them with the help of a never-ending pot of coffee. They seemed very familiar with each other, which only served to support her theory about him being a love interest. It even went so far as for him to constantly reach out and touch her hand, or move her hair out of her face where it fell while she was talking. There was nothing explicitly romantic in the gestures, but it certainly wasn't something that two people did when they had just met.

Interesting, Darcy thought. So far, she wasn't aware of any reason given for the husband's rampage yesterday, but maybe it was that he found out about her affair. That would certainly set off an episode of rage, enough to threaten a police officer with a gun to the point where she had to shoot him.

The meeting didn't last very long, probably because the man still needed to get to his job. He left first, leaving Maggie to sit and finish her pancakes.

Now that she had a new lead to follow, there was no way she was going to let it get away. Laying down a twenty dollar bill, enough for her meal and tip, she rose and followed the man out of the diner. He went back over to his car from before, and she waited and watched him leave. He turned left out of the parking lot, and she soon followed after.

As she was driving a good enough distance behind him, she dictated some notes to the recording function on her phone. "License plate number is ZB 56741. Individual appears to be a man in his late thirties or early forties, driving a red Dodge vehicle."

That was all she had to record for the moment, though she didn't dare risk looking at her phone to turn it off, which meant in the end she had twenty minutes of the sound of driving and breathing.

Then, the vehicle in front of her suddenly took a sharp right turn a few minutes outside of the shopping district. The road it took was a main outlet, but then it took another road down a smaller road. The path narrowed, the traffic dropping down to only one or two passing vehicles, so that Darcy was barely keeping the man's car in sight so he wouldn't know he was being followed.

Eventually, he turned down a private road. Glancing at her GPS, Darcy said, "Subject turned down Creek Road at 8:25 a.m."

She didn't try to follow, because a private road like that would have a gate which she couldn't follow through with the right identification or some sort of card. In any case, she didn't need to follow to still be able to track where his vehicle went. There was a gigantic building which appeared to be some sort of factory nearby, although judging by his dress she assumed he was going to be a superior or perhaps the owner of the whole thing. It was difficult to tell.

Very intriguing, she thought, and took her information home with her to look up online. She also picked up the phone and called in a favor that she'd been holding onto. While she waited for the other officer to get back to her, she quickly looked up the location o the road to see if she could find out what type of factory.

It wasn't a very difficult search. It was an automobile parts factory. A somewhat dangerous job for the lower-level workers but perhaps not so much for a man wearing a suit.

Once she found out the name of the company, the rest of it wasn't very difficult. A two-minute browse around their website showed her a link to a page with all the workers, and there was where she found him. He was wearing exactly the same sort of suit in the picture as he had been today. And his name below read Oliver Nettle.

Just then, her phone rang. It was the officer who owed her a favor. She picked it up. "What have you got for me?"

"So, the guy's name is Oliver Nettle."

I got that.

"And he's an executive manager at that auto company. The name is something stupid, like..."

"Parts of America?" she supplied.

"Yes, that's it. I guess you know that much, huh? And I checked out the plates on his car. It's been his for a little less than a year. But, he's never been in any wrecks or even pulled off any minor thefts as a kid. No drunken fights, nothing."

Maybe not as useful as I thought it was going to be.

"But, get this, okay? Weird coincidence. That guy works at the same company as the husband of that abused woman did."

"Very weird," she agreed. "I guess there wasn't much else if he doesn't have a record."

"Not really. Sorry, Darcy."

"No, thank you. I think this is exactly what I needed."

She hung up and set the phone down, and then just sat there in the dark looking at her laptop, rubbing her temples. Tomorrow when she went back to work, she would report these findings right to the Lieutenant. There was something there, some sort of answer. She knew it.

Chapter Twelve

Two days was never a very long span of time to Serena. It was hardly anything, especially during high school and the Academy. Easily forgotten. But those two days where she was out of work and just sitting at home twiddling her thumbs like a jobless deadbeat, were some of the hardest she'd ever experienced. To fill up the dreaded spare time, she put herself to the long-overdue task of cleaning up around the apartment.

That worked for a time, because it seemed like every time she thought she was done, there was still more. She turned into a cleaning fanatic for all of one day, methodically dusting the counters, organizing the cupboards, washing every piece of cloth in the house, vacuuming the carpet. She even washed all the dishes by hand.

The work lasted for most of the first day and part of the second, but then there reached a point when she was searching for a clean washcloth to wipe out the shower she just used, and she realized she was going to go in circles with this because then she would have to wash the washcloth. Getting stuck into that sort of obsessive pattern could only end badly, so she put the washcloth back up –neatly folded- and then sat down in front of the TV.

Unfortunately, most of the channels she got on her discounted service were news stations. She didn't want to hear about the problems of the world that she should be out there helping to solve and protect, so she flipped over to cartoons. They were childish and awful, a far cry from what she remembered watching as a kid, but they also somehow managed to suck her in to the point where she watched four in a row without even looking away.

Well, it was either that or she was still being affected by shock. Probably that reason.

She picked up her phone and glanced at it as soon as she came back to herself, but there were no texts waiting for her. Darcy was busy today, and oh how she wished she could also be busy.

Somehow though, eventually, she made it through. It was one of the most difficult things she had ever done, honestly. She made a cup of tea that night, though she couldn't remember ever having bought any, and put herself to bed with the tea to relax. Maybe it was the strangeness of the situation, the smell of the tea, or the ridiculousness of what she was trying to do, because it took even longer than usual for her to fall asleep.

She was woken up by her alarm in the morning. With a groan, she reached out to smack at her phone, and it took her a moment for her to realize that she had just denied a call instead of turned off an alarm she hadn't set in the first place.

“Damn,” she muttered, and sat up. Rubbing her eyes to try and see the number, she squinted. An unknown number to her. Which meant it was either nothing or it was something and Detective Flannery had tried to reach her. But, already?

That probably wasn’t a good thing. She redialed the number and waited for someone on the other line to pick up, which they did after several rings. While she was waiting, her heart started pounding more and more.

“This is Flannery,” the voice on the other end said.

“Hi, Detective Flannery,” she said. “This is Serena Blake, you just tried to call me?”

“Yes, I did.” His voice changed, but not in a way that she could glean any information from. “I need you to come on by the station today as soon as you can. We might have something.”

That was an odd way to phrase her arrest, she thought. Maybe that meant...but, no, she shouldn't let herself hope. "I'll be there very soon," she promised.

She didn't even bother with a shower, just cleaned up a little and threw her messy hair into a bun, and then drove on down to the station. The very act of just heading there started to trick her into feeling better; instead of leaning away from that sensation, she leaned on it and let it bolster her. At least she could show up looking innocent.

Once inside, she found Jacobs and Flannery waiting for her. Darcy was nowhere to be seen, which wasn't that surprising.

Lieutenant Jacobs gestured her over, ushering all three of them into her office without a word. "Okay," she said, "this is where we're at, Blake: we have some information on the wife that says she might not have given us the full story. Which means you just might be in the clear."

Her hopes soared, warm and light. "Are you serious? So soon?"

“Someone did a little unauthorized digging,” the Lieutenant answered, and from the knowing arch of her brow, Serena knew exactly who it was.

Darcy did this for me.

“Now, we can’t use it against her directly but we can manipulate it out of her if we’re good,” the detective interjected. “So what we’re going to do is interrogate her. She’s already in the break room, eating my favorite doughnut. We’ll bring her to the room and do our best to get her to confirm our suspicions.”

“So, why am I here?”

He sighed. “Because upon re-study of the pictures of the crime scene, I think I see signs of disturbance that don’t fit with the actual struggle. It’s hard to tell but it’s enough to cast doubt. And in this job, when you have doubt, you act on it. So, my hide is resting on this just as much as yours is.”

Serena doubted that. A wrong analysis on his part was nothing compared to the ruination of her whole career.

A few minutes later and Serena was standing in front of the two-way mirror through which she could see into the room, but through which Maggie couldn't see out. The interrogation room was sparse, with a table and a couple of chairs. Maggie sat at one side of the table, while Detective Flannery perched at the other; Lieutenant Jacobs stood by the door, still as a statue so that it was hard to notice her at first tucked away in the shadows like that.

Her whole career rested on this. How sad was it that she didn't think she was going to be able to walk out of here with a badge?

"So," Flannery said comfortably, "thank you for coming back here, ma'am. I know it can't be easy for you to have to do this but we need all the information we can get."

"I already told you everything," Maggie said softly, her voice quavering. Serena watched her intently. She had *saved* that woman. How on earth could she do this to her? The man had been abusing her, for fuck's sake!

"Yes, but sometimes we remember new information later on," he said, his voice gentle but firm. The woman looked caught and timid, making her wince. "There was no one else in the house with you that night?"

Maggie looked absolutely abashed. "Anyone with me that night? What are you saying, that I was cheating on Thomas?"

"It would hardly be cheating at that point though, but that wasn't what I was asking."

It was hard to tell through the dark window, but she thought she saw the Detective's eyes narrow. Jacobs also shifted her posture, though that could have been for a variety of reasons.

"So, there was no one in the house?"

"No one!"

"But, do you know anyone who might have wanted to check on you? Any friends? Co-workers? Neighbors who might just want to drop by?"

Maggie shook her head. "I don't work. And Thomas didn't like it when I went out with my friends, so I just...don't have any. And I don't talk to the neighbors either."

"No one from your husband's work?"

"I don't know anyone who worked at the company," she said.

"Hmm," Flannery murmured. "You see, Maggie, I'm not sure I believe that. You know that we've had officers following you around the past few days to make sure you're safe."

She nodded rapidly. "Oh yes. And I really appreciate it."

"Then, it might not come as a surprise to you that our officers have seen you have breakfast with someone the past couple days."

"So?" she said. And her voice had changed. It was no longer sweet, but turned defensive and stark. Serena leaned in so close that her nose almost bumped the glass. Only a hand on her shoulder, restraining her, prevented her from doing so.

Darcy, she thought, turning to look at her former partner.

Darcy nodded at her and they both went back to watching.

"You see, we have learned that the man you have been meeting with is from your husband's work. An executive manager, as I'm sure you know. You don't dress in a suit to go pull levers and check a conveyor belt."

Maggie's face blanched, slowly leeching of color.

"So, I have to wonder...That's a lie, Maggie. What else have you lied about?"

Maggie looked down at her hands, clearly resistant, but then broke only a few seconds later. "Fine!" she sobbed. "Fine!"

"Tell the truth," Lieutenant Jacobs said, stepping forward from her place by the door. Even being only of moderate height, her impressive stature and posed bearing were enough to push Maggie over the edge.

"Fine!" she sobbed again. "Thomas never abused me. But he was suspicious. I loved Oliver ever since I saw him. We were great together. And then Thomas came home and caught us in bed together. Oliver ran out and Thomas hit me."

"But you hit him back," Flannery said, and whipped out a photograph. From where she was at the door, Serena could just barely tell that it was probably a picture of the husband's corpse on the coroner's table. "Didn't you?"

"Yes."

So, a fight. Not abuse. Never abuse.

"And what about the gun? He had one, didn't he?"

"Yes. He did. He was so mad...I locked him out of the room but he was hitting it and saying he was going to shoot the lock and I was scared so I called the police. And then he came in and I hit him with the umbrella stand. And then that officer girl was waiting for me."

"Right," Flannery said, and waved his hand a little. "We know all about that. But what I'm very curious about is to where the gun went."

"Oliver told me he came back in and hid it for me," Maggie said bitterly. "The life insurance policy the company officers is huge but I wouldn't get any of it if Thomas died committing suicide or if he had a criminal record. The neighbors were going to call the cops on us I just know it. And then I never would have gotten *anything*. And Oliver loves me and wanted me to be rich. So he hid the gun and told me, and I lied about it. Fuck."

Serena turned away from the window, shaking a little bit. "I can't believe it," she muttered. "I really can't believe it. She tried to frame me. After I saved her."

Darcy wrapped her arm comfortingly around her shoulders. "Yes, she did try to frame you. I'm sorry, Serena. But what do you say we go into the break room, get some coffee, and wait to hear the final verdict?"

An hour later, Lieutenant Jacobs came into the room. Serena sat restlessly with Darcy at a table covered in empty coffee cups, which she was currently stacking while the older cop shredded another into a spiral.

"Blake?" Jacobs said firmly.

She practically leapt up to her feet. "Yes, Lieutenant?"

Her stern face cracked down the middle and she held out her hand, grinning broadly. "All charges against you have been dropped. Maggie and her boy-toy Oliver are being arrested for conspiracy against the police as we speak. You're in the clear."

"Thank you," Serena stammered, and then she did the only thing left to do: burst into grateful tears.

Chapter Thirteen

That night, Serena drove her cruiser home and left the truck at the station. It felt so unbelievably good to have the job car back, so good that she couldn't bear not to have it nearby. Her heart soared. She rolled the windows down, let her hair out of the restraining bun, and pretended she was in a sports car. Life was that good.

It was a different story when she got home, though. The happiness nestled in her chest was struggling to warm her cold bones, and she sat down on the couch in her living room with a disbelieving little sound. And then she put her head in her hands, making another tiny sound as she thought of how close she had come to losing everything she worked so hard for. But now she would get to stay and keep her brother's memory alive with many more years at the force. So many twists and turns that she hardly knew what she thought.

Someone knocked at her door. "It's Darcy," Darcy called, and then she let herself in. Serena looked up just a little bit, peeking between her fingers at the older cop.

She looked exactly the same as when they met, yet she herself felt ten times as rough, and forty years older. "How on earth do you do this?" she whispered.

Darcy perched on the couch beside her, and then leaned against her side to lay her head on her shoulder. The gesture surprised her, but it felt good. Good and right. Just like before.

It really was a mistake to let go of you, wasn't it? Damn. I've done so many stupid things...

"You're really going to have to be more specific, babe."

"How do you keep going? After something like this?"

Darcy shook her head a little so that her hair tickled on Serena's neck. Incredibly, something warm started to tingle between her legs. She could hardly believe it. She had been so detached from herself the past several days, and now the first thing she really felt again was her pussy. "Honestly, Serena. Do you think you're the only cop to ever get herself involved in a scandal? It wasn't even that bad, and it wasn't your fault. You haven't lost anything. *That* is how you're going to get over it, okay? It's no big deal at all, I promise. Okay?"

"You ever get into trouble like this?" Serena asked bitterly. "Be honest."

"Sure! Jacobs almost canned my ass when I started to fuck one of the rookies I was training."

She laughed. "So, what did you do?"

"I waited until she wasn't a rookie anymore. Sometimes we just have to wait." A comforting hand petted the back of her neck, gently soothing her. "Sometimes, you just need to wait. No one will remember this in a month. Neither will you."

But I think these nightmares will last me a lifetime.

She didn't bring that up, though. And she thought Darcy might be avoiding the subject, too.

Meanwhile, there was another subject which needed quite a lot of attention. "I know that you're the officer who did all the investigating, you know."

"I was."

"Thank you."

“That’s what you do for the people who love you.” The short-haired cop shrugged.

Serena blurted out, “I love you, too.” And there it was. Everything she had been afraid of, the words she had been afraid to commit to before, were all out in the open now. She couldn’t hide from them.

“Prove it.”

Serena wiggled her body, bumping her hip teasingly against Darcy’s, dislodging her from her shoulder. And then she turned, lay her hand along the other woman’s beautiful cheekbone, and leaned in for a kiss.

Their lips met very sweetly, teasing and rubbing together. Serena whimpered as the tingles in her pussy deepened and gained intensity, making her wet. Darcy’s fingers tangled in her hair, pulling at large handfuls of it to get their lips moving together harder and with more passion than before.

"Fuck, I love you, Darcy," Serena whimpered, her hips squirming around so hard in her arousal that she practically climbed into the other woman's lap. Her lips parted, allowing Darcy's tongue entrance. Warm and wet met sweet and begging, their tongues playing together and mimicking the very act of lovemaking.

"I love you, too," Darcy murmured against her lips. "But you still haven't proven it yet. Are you sure you want to do this with me?"

"More sure than I've been of anything in the past week," she replied, and started tugging at her clothes. Her need was beyond controllable now, but her efforts weren't getting her very far. "I want to try."

Darcy gently knocked her hands away and began to undo the buttons and straps of her uniform, teasingly pulling away each garment and dropping them to the side as slowly as she could.

"Darcy!" Serena whined. The moment she was down to her bra and dampened panties, she wriggled up fully onto the other woman's lap and kissed her hard, and then redoubled her efforts at undressing –but this time, she was undressing Darcy.

They were trembling and shaking from kissing and teasing each other by the time they were both fully undressed. And then they kissed again, so hard that Serena felt her lips bruise from being crushed. The sting was nothing, thrown into the pot along with all the other sensations coursing through her body.

And as the warmth and adrenaline of sex flooded through her, she felt the weariness and chill of the day leave her body. Later on it would be back, but right now she would cling to it and wring as much enjoyment from it as she could.

Somehow, she found herself kneeling on the floor between Darcy's spread legs, looking up into the other woman's sparkling eyes. "Is it finally my turn to please you?"

"Go right ahead, babe."

Although she'd seen her own plenty of times, Serena had never had a chance to look at it from this angle. At first glance, she had no idea what to make of it. It looked nothing like what it *felt* like. Actually, it kind of looked a bit intimidating.

"It's very nice to feel you breathe on me," Darcy murmured, stroking her hair again, "but I wish you'd stop teasing me like that."

"I've just....never seen one before. It's...confusing?"

"What's confusing?" Darcy asked. She let go of Serena's hair with one hand and reached down to stroke a finger across her pussy lips. "Look, it's like a flower. These are my outer petals. They get big and swollen when I'm happy to draw you in." She started to slide her finger past her lips. "And these are my inner folds. This is where the pollen is. Be a little bee and come get it, won't you?"

Serena laughed, and her rush of hot breath on Darcy's pussy must have aroused her, because the other woman gasped and jumped a little. "Oh!"

Her own pussy growing more excited, feeling empowered by what she was able to do, Serena moved the other woman's hand out of the way. She was so excited as she stretched out her tongue to stroke it across her outer lips.

Like any woman, she had tasted herself once or twice but it was never anything like this. Somehow the texture of the other woman made her a thousand times sweeter and the moment she began she felt Darcy's juices start to really flow into her mouth. Sticking out her tongue a little further, she tried to catch them all.

"Fuck, Serena...Suck me a little, okay?"

How am I supposed to do that? she wondered.

Searching around a little, she eventually decided to open her mouth against the other woman's pussy. The position felt awkward as hell but then she tried sucking, and was rewarded with a mouthful of hot juices, and Darcy bucking her pussy at her mouth with a soft scream.

I did that. I did that to her.

Encouraged, she started sucking on her pussy even harder, alternating long and short pulls, and making sure to make plenty of sloppy-wet sounds. Her own pussy started throbbing as she felt Darcy shake and tremble beneath her. Then, she remembered how the other cop had done it, and opened her mouth a little wider so that her upper lip started to hit and torture her clit.

“Fuck yes!” Darcy cried out. “Fuck me now! Tongue-fuck me! Make me cum!”

Obediently, Serena thrust out her tongue right into Darcy’s throbbing folds. In an instant, the other woman’s muscles tightened around hers, and her back arched. Serena gripped her beneath her ass with her nails, riding her pussy with her mouth as she shook and her cum filled her mouth.

Eagerly, Serena swallowed most of it but kept some of it in her mouth to come up and share with Darcy so she could taste herself.

“Fuck,” Darcy murmured. “Where the fuck did you learn how to do that? You said you’re not a lesbian.”

“I...I’ve done oral a time or two,” Serena admitted, blushing.

Darcy laughed. “You’re so cute.”

“But anyway, I am a lesbian now.” She beamed up into Darcy’s beautiful eyes. “Your lesbian.”

“That’s not quite how it works.”

“Maybe not,” she admitted, “but we’re cops. We can bend the rules if it’s for the greater good.”

Darcy shook her head. “That’s also not how it works.”

“Darcy!” she complained. “Let me have my fun, okay?”

“Oh, I will,” the other woman purred, and grabbed her around the waist to turn her over and lay her back against the couch. Then, she began to slide down to the floor. “Now, stay right there and I’ll give you just as much fun as you can handle...”

Closing her eyes and leaning back, Serena reflected on how different things were now than only a few months ago. Looking back on herself, she saw all the things she wished she’d done differently, and could only hope that her brother was proud of her, wherever she was.

Most importantly, she hoped Darcy was proud of her. She intended to be the best birthday present every for quite a long time.

The End

About the Author

Carmen Lace is a romance author living in the Pacific Northwest. It is true, it does rain a lot in the Pacific Northwest, but that gives her the right atmosphere to be creative and write her stories. A quiet rainy night by the fireplace with her computer is a perfect setting for her. When she is not busy writing, she loves escaping in a book, traveling, and just enjoying life with friends and family.

Please visit her website and subscribe to her newsletter where she announce new books coming out and give out free promotions/books (she hates spam herself and have total respect for subscribers). Again thank you for downloading this book and look forward to reading your feedback on Amazon.

Download one of her other books for FREE:
http://carmenlace.com/giveaway